LOCKED IN FEMININITY

3

A Feminized and Emasculated Sissy

Lady Alexa

Copyright © Lady Alexa 2021
1st Edition

All rights reserved. No reproduction, copy or transmission of this publication or section in this publication may be reproduced, copied or transmitted without written permission of the author.

This novel is a work of fiction. Names, characters, businesses, places, events and incidents are either the products of the author's imagination or used in a fictitious manner. Any resemblance to actual persons, living or dead, or actual events is purely coincidental.

This novel contains explicit scenes of a sexual nature including forced male to female gender change, female domination, humiliation, CFNM, spanking and reluctant feminisation. All characters in this story are aged 18 and over.

Strictly for adults aged 18 and over or the age of maturity in your country.

Subscribe to my blog and newsletter and receive special offers, free articles and stories.

Go to www.ladyalexauk.com and enter your email address into the newsletter box in the sidebar.

CONTENTS

Chapter 1 – It's A Sissy's Life

Chapter 2 – Sissy At Work

Chapter 3 – Change of Plan

Chapter 4 – Sell-Out

Chapter 5 — The New Plan

Chapter 6 – Relief

Chapter 7 – Consequences

Chapter 8 – Chastity in Pink

Chapter 9 — Locked and Loaded

Chapter 10 —Reunion

Chapter 11 – The Mistress Dinner Party Affair

Chapter 12 —The Breast of Friends

Chapter 13 —It Must be Love, Love, Love

Chapter 14 – Cum Again

Chapter 15 — Satisfying Polly

Chapter 16 — What's the Story Morning Glory?

Chapter 17 — The Future's Bright, The Future's Pink

Lockdown Feminization may be read as a standalone novel but you will get more from the story if you first read Lockdown Feminization 1 and 2.

Chapter 1 – It's A Sissy's Life

David pulled the pink cloth facemask over his nose; the word *Girl* was printed across the front. He rested his slim hands on the top of his short white pleated miniskirt. He tapped long pink glossy fingernails on the light fabric. The skirt was so light, the faintest whiff of breeze caused it to billow around his legs like a gossamer sail.

Aunt Ruth insisted he dress in the most feminine colours and prettiest and shortest skirts. Especially for his first day at work in her factory. She wanted him to make an impression. That much was guaranteed. Exposed and embarrassed were two sensations that closed around him.

His light-tan stockings glistened in the milky morning sunlight as it streamed through the reception-area windows. He tapped the soles of high-heeled sandals on the marble flooring in impatience. He didn't like waiting dressed like this in such an open space. He guessed it would get worse. People went to and fro in and out of the building. Their eyes burnt into him. Even if they hadn't spotted he was a man, his girly clothing drew their stares.

He wiped the back of his hand across his forehead, careful not to smudge the smokey blue eye makeup. He unzipped the front of his white leather waist-length jacket in the warmth of the lobby. His pink blouse with a wide frill down the front and large mother-of-pearl buttons showed. He pushed a hand under his jacket shoulder to pull up a fallen strap of his bra without thinking.

He kept his legs tight together, knees touching and to one side. He'd had to learn this to avoid his skimpy white panties and tell-tale bulge showing. His bulge wasn't that big but in small tight panties, it didn't need to be.

The lobby of Aunt Ruth's factory was soulless and corporate. The factory used to produce the clothing range for her company, Amey Apparel Ltd. Aunt Ruth was not his blood relative. In truth, he wasn't even his aunt any more; his father's brother, Robert, had died the previous year. David had never met his aunt until she had sought him out as the only living blood relative of her now-deceased husband.

Someday this company would all be his, assuming everything went to plan. He had to play Aunt Ruth's game for a short time. He had to do what his aunt told him or lose his inheritance and the chance to become rich. He'd do anything to get rich but hadn't anticipated his aunt's passionate desire to make up for lost time in not having her own daughter or niece. If that's what it took to get his hands on her money, then that's what he'd do. It wasn't as if he didn't have the experience as a sissy.

After he'd left Ms Lipman's employment as her personal sissy, he hadn't expected Aunt Ruth to embrace his feminisation with such enthusiasm. Or for her to expect him to continue to call her Aunt even though his uncle was dead and she was no longer a real aunt. The problem was she wanted him to be the niece she'd never had. The fact he was male was a minor detail for Aunt Ruth. She planned to rectify that small problem. It hadn't helped that Ms Lipman had already transformed him into a sissy. He was halfway there. Maybe more.

His fingers lay between the sharp pleats of the pretty little tennis-style skirt. He crossed his legs. His penis pushed out in the light panties almost showing beneath the hem of the skirt. Something stirred inside him at that sensation. He tugged on the little pleated tennis skirt in an attempt to cover himself. The frilly top of the hold-up stockings still showed, it was futile.

He pulled the shoulder strap of his small white leather shoulder bag over his head. He placed it next to him on the sofa. He adjusted the pink face mask again and rubbed on his smooth exposed thighs. His chest felt tight, not only from the bra. His head thumped. He wiped his forehead again and kept his eyes on the floor, avoiding eye contact and the risk of someone noticing he was male. That situation was not going to last long. He wanted to curl up and hide or to run away. He wouldn't run far in the four-inch heels.

If he'd thought he would be able to hide away during the Covid crisis, he soon learned that wasn't going to happen. She wanted him to learn about her business by working for her. And she wanted him to live as a pretty sissy girl for everyone to see.

He could expect no favours; he had to start work at the bottom. As she had started out, she'd told him. That wasn't true: Aunt Ruth had never worked in a factory.

"You've had your Covid vaccinations. With a pretty pink facemask you'll be perfectly safe," she had told him before reminding him to wash his hands regularly and carry hand sanitiser in his shoulder bag.

He twirled a finger through his long luxurious blond hair. The factory was in an anonymous business park on the edge of town. He'd travelled by taxi but Aunt Ruth told him that was only because it was his first day. He needed to learn about costs and to be frugal; it would be the bus from tomorrow.

A lanyard hung around his neck and over the pink blouse. A laminated credit-card like security badge hung from the lanyard. It read, *Guest*. The middle-aged male security guard's had locked his eyes on David's long slim legs, not noticing his true sex. David may be small and slim but his face had something masculine. David shuddered.

Clipping urgent footsteps approached him and stopped. He looked up. A tall lady in a dark suit and shoulder-length straightened brown hair looked down on him. He swallowed hard. She put out a hand and a strained smile. He shook her fingers with a light grip. She grimaced.

"You'll be Primrose, I presume," said the lady. "Ruth described you perfectly." Her nose turned up as if a nasty smell had appeared.

David gulped hard. Aunt Ruth had said that if she'd had a daughter she would have called her Primrose. Now she had a niece, the name Primrose was perfect. His previous mistresses used to call him Amy. Aunt Ruth said she didn't like the thought of him being Amy Amey. She had a point.

He stood and was shorter than the lady, even in his four-inch heels. "Yes, that's me," he croaked, eyes down and hating the idea of admitting he was called Primrose. Think of the millions, he told himself.

"I'm Amanda Sharpe, Head of Marketing at Amey Apparel." Her nose screwed again up for a moment. She looked him over before returning to neutrality. "You were to become my secretary. However, after speaking to your aunt, we decided it would be better to put you to work in the factory. That way you can get an idea of how the operation works at ground level. You may graduate to become a secretary in the future." She looked him over again. "You're never going to be able to move that needle on our value-added business model if you don't know the basics."

David stared hard at her. What was she talking about? Ground level? Moving needles? Business model? The words were English but made no sense.

"I'm going to introduce you to the other workers." She assessed David again as if not believing her eyes. "I'm sure your aunt explained. We've turned the factory over to the manufacture of masks and protective medical clothing during this pandemic. It's a short-term but lucrative option. Besides, people don't need so many clothes if they're not going out, do they, Primrose?"

"No, Amanda," David said without understanding what the hell she was on about. He looked around everywhere but at her hard stare.

Clothing, masks, medical products? It was irrelevant, it all sounded like hard work. He didn't like that idea.

"Primrose," said Amanda Sharpe.

David looked up at her and shivered. Primrose. How humiliating. "Yes?" he croaked.

"I know you're Ruth's nephew. Niece, I suppose." The corner of her lip twitched, suppressing a smile. "But when you're working here, you'll call me Ms Sharpe. Is that clear, Primrose?"

"But."

"No buts, Primrose, these were Ruth's instructions. We will not treat you any differently to the other girls."

David looked away and outside. Girls? "OK, Ms Sharpe."

"Good girl. Follow me."

Amanda Sharpe turned and marched towards a set of double blue doors to the side of the reception desk. She didn't look to see if he was following. David followed.

He'd been feminised for several weeks, but it had been largely indoors and in front of a limited number of people. Now he was about to meet his aunt's manufacturing employees. All one hundred and twenty-three of them.

The things he had to do to get his inheritance. It would be more than worth the humiliation in the end. He'd be a multi-millionaire and then he could do whatever he wanted. Returning to being a male would be the first option.

Chapter 2 – Sissy at Work

David's face burned like red-hot coals.

He stood next to Ms Sharpe on a small raised step in front of a crowd of factory floor workers. Most were women. Ms Sharpe was speaking and making the situation worse.

"This pretty little thing is David Amey."

David gasped. Had she said pretty little thing? He scanned the surgical masked crowd. They looked on with amused interest and several low-volume discussions were going on.

"David is Ruth Amey's nephew. I know he looks like a girl." She looked at him with amusement. "Well, almost. Anyway, we call her Primrose."

A wave of sniggers flowed.

"Treat him as if he were a real girl. It's what she wants."

David didn't know whether if the word *she* was about him or Aunt Ruth. A wave of discussion began among the workers.

"He, I mean she," Ms Sharpe put a crooked finger to her lips and giggled. "Silly me. *She* will start with the cutting team." She turned to David. "You'll be working on cutting out the medical masks from sheets of fabric." She stepped off the raised step as the entire audience gawked at David. "This way, Primrose. Good girl." She strode away as before without looking back.

The crowd stood aside as Ms Sharpe strode to an area in the corner of the large rectangular factory building. Her heels echoed on the hard concrete floor like a marching soldier. David staggered after her, the eyes of every employee on him. His skirt flowed against the tops of his thighs as he walked. He loved that feeling, but not right at that moment.

Ms Sharpe reached a yellow sign that said cutting machines and turned. She folded her arms and pursed her bright red lips. David caught up with her, followed by around twenty women and a young man. They crowded around David in a semi-circle.

"Janice is the forelady, she'll show you what to do, Primrose," said Ms Sharpe and she walked away. She was gone in seconds.

David faced a circle of inquisitive staring eyes.

"Are you a man or a girl? Or a transvestite?" said a middle-aged lady in a tee-shirt and jeans, her mask under her double chin like a blue beard.

David coughed, looked away. "Yes." He kept his pink mask up, it offered some degree of anonymity.

The group laughed.

"Do you still have a willy?" It was a young woman's voice, hard and high pitched and it rang around the factory floor. She brushed a hand through green spiky hair.

David felt dizzy. "Yes, of course I have one."

The green-haired woman looked down at his crotch area. "Prove it, girly-boy."

David blushed bright red. She pushed two palms against a small slim young man. "You'd have to use Primrose's back passage, Stevie."

It was the turn of the young man in the group to blush.

The green-haired lady pushed Stevie again. "Or maybe you'd like to suck on Primrose's dick, Stevie?"

Stevie tapped at her arm, red-cheeked and creased face. "I'm not gay, Sharon."

More laughter. She looked back at Stevie. "I know you're not, but Primrose isn't a man. She's a girl with a dick." The laughter continued.

A middle-aged lady approached David and put her arm around him. "I'm Janice, dearie. Don't mind them. I'll show you how to cut the masks. They'll soon get bored of teasing you."

She took David's hand and led him to the cutting machine. Getting through this to receive his inheritance had become a whole lot harder.

Janice had been right, the workers at the factory lost interest in teasing David. He noticed the males would shoot a look at his slim legs. He ignored them and learnt how to cut the masks. It wasn't that hard, even for him. It was simple and repetitive which made things better. Easy was good for him. Janice told him what he had to do. He preferred someone telling him what to do, it saved having to think too much.

As he worked, he reminded himself that Aunt Ruth was in her sixties and tired of running the business, especially now Uncle Robert had died. It was a matter of time before she handed the company over to him. He didn't want to run a company, that sounded too much like hard work. Once he took over, he'd sell it and live off the money, throw off this forced femininity and never work again. That was a great plan.

He smiled as he cut the masks out. Life was going to be wonderful; he had to be patient. A few months more. That's all it would take. It shouldn't take too long, what could ever go wrong?

Chapter 3 – Change of Plan

"I'm holding a board meeting tomorrow afternoon, Primrose." Aunt Ruth sat at the head of the dining table, she leant back in her chair. She blinked red-lined eyes.

It was Friday evening and he'd been working at her factory for three months. They dined alone, Aunt Ruth had given her cook the night off and prepared dinner for both of them. That was unusual, especially as he hadn't seen her much recently. She'd been working in her home office late most nights. Aunt Ruth was restrained, that wasn't like her. It was as if she had something to say but was looking for the right moment.

David sat on her right. He wore a short yellow chiffon ra-ra skirt which rode up and he brushed it back down. It clicked with static sparks over the tan shiny stockings. The dining room doubled as an auxiliary meeting room; the table was more like a large meeting room table. A massive TV screen hung on a wall at the far end giving the area more of the feel of a corporate area.

Aunt Ruth had come down from her office earlier in the evening. She'd pulled his blond hair back from his face and tucked a white Alice band in. This was a new innovation. The hairdressers were closed due to the epidemic; he hadn't been unable to get his cut or styled; it hung long and straight down to the small of his back. The new weight was nice, as was the way it bounced when he walked or swayed his head. He hadn't expected that.

His fringe fell to his chin, hence the Alice band now clipped onto the top of his head. He was pleased the hairdressers were shut but hadn't told Aunt Ruth that. Aunt Ruth was planning to take him to a female salon. The longer this trip was delayed the better.

Aunt Ruth always managed to keep her hair tidy, despite the lack of open hairdressers. She ironed it dead straight, a uniform mid-brown to her shoulders. She brushed it back and her small neat ears showed. Large white pearl stud earrings were in each lobe.

"I'm going to have a meeting tomorrow. By Zoom, of course," Aunt Ruth said. "It's frustrating we still can't meet in person because of this damn pandemic." She put down her knife and fork and raised an eyebrow. "Amanda Sharpe will be coming in person though, she lives nearby."

He remembered Ms Sharpe from his first day at the factory those three months ago. He'd not seen her since.

"Why are you having a meeting at the weekend, Aunt Ruth? What's going on?"

Aunt Ruth placed her fork on the table. She chewed slowly, her eyes red and sore. "I'm making major changes to the company." Ruth looked over his face. "And because of these changes, today was your last day at the factory."

His face lit up. This was damn good news. He wouldn't miss the journey on the bus dressed like a bimbo. Nor having to work. Work was, well, hard work; he preferred laying in bed and watching TV. Finally, he might be getting an executive role of some kind, telling other people to do the work. That sounded fun.

"Am I going to be working for Ms Sharpe now?"

Amanda was tall and posh, but sexy. Amanda reminded him of his first female boss, the American lawyer, Anne Dufort. Hot, confident and bossy. He liked those traits in a woman. Especially he liked bossy for some reason. It made him tingle. Amanda was bossy.

Ruth rubbed her eyes with the palm of her hand. "No, Primrose, you won't be working for Amanda." She thought for a moment. "I have other plans for you."

Other plans? That could be good or bad. "What plans, Aunt Ruth?" he said, expecting good news.

"All in good time, Primrose. What I can say is your progress has not been fast enough for me. I have been neglecting your development. You have stagnated and you have so much potential and so much to offer. I'll be making the time to deal with that." She stroked his cheek with a single finger, kindness etched in her tired eyes. He loved it when she was loving to him.

He sat up straighter as her words sank in. Potential? Development? Time? Did she now see him as CEO material after all? How could that be? He'd been working at the factory as an assembly worker. He'd had no chance to do anything other than cut out facemasks on a machine. He saw her studying his face and blushed. She was old but damn sexy. Was that wrong? She wasn't a real aunt so he guessed not.

"Don't worry about that for now, Primrose-Petal. We need to get through the board meeting first then I'll be able to concentrate on what I want for you."

Petal? He cringed in embarrassment but his penis tingled at what she'd said. He studied his peas, an excuse to recover and his blush to recede. At least he wouldn't have to work at the factory any more. "So what will I be doing at the Zoom meeting?"

Aunt Ruth cut into her dinner. "Nothing. But as you're named in Robert's will, you have to be there when the changes are confirmed, according to my lawyer." She grimaced. "Unfortunately."

He looked down. This seemed demeaning. "What decision, Aunt Ruth?"

She shook her straight brown hair back with a twist of her head. It moved as one unit. Fuck me, she was hot, he thought. He wouldn't have used that word out loud with Aunt Ruth. She wouldn't be amused. *Swearing is an excuse for an inability to find the correct words to correctly articulate your feelings*, she would tell him. Aunt Ruth spoke a different language to normal people. One that made little sense to David.

She rubbed both hands down her face, stretching the bottoms of her raw eyes. "I told you I don't want to discuss it." The sudden snappy response exposed her weariness. "I want to relax over dinner, to enjoy my niece looking more feminine by the day," she said, sitting up straighter. "You'll find out tomorrow what's going on so stop quizzing me, Princess. I'm tired and I still have a lot of preparation for tomorrow's meeting. I have contracts to read in detail." She sighed. "It's stressful and tiring running a company, it never stops. I'm not getting any younger." She studied him a moment. "Not that you'd understand," she snapped.

It was unusual for Aunt Ruth to be uptight, she was normally controlled. She'd been working too hard. At least after tomorrow's board meeting, she could relax a little and take the time to be nicer with him. He liked that and when she stroked his face or tidied his hair.

But what was this meeting about and why did he have to be there for the decision? Why was her lawyer involved? And why had she started calling him her niece more often and using female pet-names? Petal? Princess? His penis hardened at the thought.

Chapter 4 – Sell-Out

David sat to Aunt Ruth's left in the dining-come-meeting room. Outside the wind blew and spits of rain hit the windows; a storm was brewing up. Low dark-grey clouds covered the sky. It was early afternoon but the ceiling lights glowed bright in the gloom.

David stood and switched on the large TV monitor with a black remote control. The display burst into life and the and the picture showed a screen divided in two. Aunt Ruth and him on one side and Amanda Sharpe on the other. Amanda was sitting to his aunt's right, an open white laptop sat in front of her on the table. She looked over his smooth legs and his short flared pink skirt. He sat down under her stare and her smirk increased.

The TV screen divided further and four more faces appeared on the screen. Two were in the same room and wearing surgical face masks. The other two were in different offices with books lined up behind them on crammed shelving.

Aunt Ruth cleared her throat. "Perfect, all on time." She looked across at Amanda as David fidgeted in his seat. "Welcome everyone and thank you for giving up your Saturday afternoon to conclude this business," said Aunt Ruth. "I have Amanda Sharpe here with me, Marketing Director Amey Apparel plc. I can see on screen we have Patricia Hodge, Amey Apparel's Chief Counsel who is at the HQ of Bedizen plc with John Hopwood, Bedizen Chief Counsel. And a special welcome to Clive Dankworth, CEO Bedizen."

A series of hellos sounded out. Patricia and John were sitting at a small round table in a modern office. Tall office buildings rose behind them through large windows. Behind Clive, a large bookshelf was stacked with rows of management books lining the shelves. Several books were not business books but by an aristocrat called Lady Alexa. David saw *The Female Species, A Sister-in-Law's Law* and *Becoming Joanne* titles behind the CEO on the screen. David guessed he must be well connected to know an aristocrat. These were important people, thought David: But what was going on?

"And we also have my nephew, David Amey, here."

David cringed at Aunt Ruth using nephew to introduce him. He'd hoped over the TV screen they would have not noticed he wasn't a real girl. The eyes on the screen widened seeing David's face, his full make-up, long blond hair and the white Alice band. His pink blouse was open-necked with large collars and a wide frill down the front,

Clive Dankworth leant forward, his grey hair short and parted on the side. It was gelled down flat. He could have been anywhere between forty or sixty. He wore the businessman uniform of a bold blue and white striped shirt, open at the neck.

"David you say, Ruth?" said Clive, his face creased in surprise.

David wanted to hunch up and disappear into the floor. Ruth looked at him. "Sit up Primrose."

He sat up with a start. The faces on the screen continued to stare, Clive's mouth dropped open.

Ruth smiled at David and turned to the screen. "We will use the name David today for legal reasons due to the nature of this conference call." She looked back at David and stroked his head and ran a hand down the back to his neck. She left it there. "These days she prefers to go by Primrose. Primrose Amey. Legally, she's still a male. For now." She creased her eyes in a tired smile. "A pretty little thing, don't you think?"

David reddened and his body burned with heat at the humiliation his aunt was putting him through. He closed his eyes.

"Yes, indeed." Clive's voice came over the speaker. "Shall we get on?"

Aunt Ruth straightened. "Yes, of course, Clive. It seemed pertinent to explain Primrose's situation."

She shuffled the papers laying on the table in front of her. David thought she appeared nervous, delaying. That was odd, not like her at all.

"Patricia, John. Are you satisfied with the contract?"

Patricia leant into the screen and looked to John Hopwood. "Yes we have agreed on the wording and we are good to go."

"Excellent." Aunt Ruth's voice wavered. "Clive? Good for you?"

"Yes," said Clive. "I'm ready to transfer the £150M."

"What's going on Aunt Ruth?" asked David.

She raised a finger in his face. "Shush, Primrose, don't be a naughty girl. I told you to keep quiet. You're only here for legal reasons."

What reasons, he wanted to shout?

Aunt Ruth faced to her right. "Amanda?"

Amanda nodded. David realised at that point she was his Aunt Ruth's de facto number two.

"Let's do it," said Aunt Ruth.

On-screen, Patricia and John shook hands and passed folders to each other. Clive nodded to someone off-screen. Amanda peered into her laptop. After a few moments, she nodded at Aunt Ruth. "Funds received."

"It's done. Congratulations to everyone," said Aunt Ruth. Her voice sounded low, her up-beat manner forced.

"What's done, Aunt Ruth?" asked David.

She looked to him and touched his arm tenderly and her finger remained on his forearm. He tingled at her touch as her face softened. "I've sold Amey Apparel, Princess."

Chapter 5 —The New Plan

The call closed with everyone congratulating each other. Except for David. He scraped the chair back and flounced out of the room, his long hair bobbing. He stomped up the stairs to his bedroom and slammed the door behind him. How could Aunt Ruth pull the rug away from under him? Aunt Ruth left him to stew alone.

Hunger beat him after three hours and he wandered downstairs and into the kitchen. It was early evening. He was still sulking. Ruth sat at the small table nursing a small brandy. She stared up at David, eyes cold, unblinking. "It wasn't going to work, Primrose. You'd never be ready to take over the company."

It was as if he saw banknotes flying away. "But Uncle Robert's will left the company to me once you stopped wanting to run it."

"Yes."

"You can't sell the company, you have to leave it to me. You've broken the law."

"No."

"No?"

"No."

"How, why?" Desperation caught in his throat. This couldn't be happening. His plan had collapsed around him.

Ruth looked away. "There was a clause."

His mouth dropped open. He closed it again. "What? What does that mean?"

"As I said, you're not up to running a company. Not only did you not bother to read the will, you don't know what a clause is which proves my point."

"Tell me what you're talking about, Aunt Ruth." He stamped a desperate foot on the tiled floor. His little skirt flounced around his thigh.

She breathed out and closed her eyes for a moment. "You make a pretty girl, Primrose." She shook her head. "A clause is a separate part of a contract, or a will, that adds an exception to that contract. Or will."

He listened, his mouth dry, trying to process her words. He hated it when things got technical.

Ruth watched him and carried on. "The clause states that Amey Holdings Ltd will only be left to you if I decide not to sell. You're completely unsuitable and I see no way you'd ever be ready. You take after your father; you're lazy and not that bright. I'm sixty-two and I want to retire. I can't leave it to you to run so I sold up."

His entire future was unravelling. He'd endured the three months working at his aunt's factory making Covid masks dressed as a bimbo for nothing. He held his palms to his eyes and rubbed away the first tears.

A thought came to him. He pulled his hands away from his face. "You told me the will said I had to do whatever you told me if I wanted to get the company. You wanted me as the daughter or niece you never had." David folded his arms in triumph. "That means I don't have to follow your stupid rules any more. So. I'm going to be a man again and you can't stop me. And I don't want to be your stupid niece either."

Aunt Ruth shook her head. "Primrose Petal. Luckily you make such a pretty girl as your brainpower is limited. Which is the problem and the solution."

David opened his mouth and shut it again. Did she just imply he was stupid? He'd show her. "You're not so clever yourself, Aunt Ruth. Selling the company and losing me as your niece."

She raised her eyebrows. "And why would that be, Princess?"

His lips tightened. "Because now you've sold the company, I don't have to do what you tell me. And I will not be a girl for you any more." He stood tall. "Ha, put that in your pipe and smoke it. Ruth, not Aunt. And stop calling me Primrose. Or Princess. Or Petal."

Aunt Ruth threw her head back and laughed. "Oh pretty pouting Princess Petal, you're so funny. "I have £150M in the bank and the same rule applies."

he was finding his aunt annoying. "What rule?" he asked, wondering where this was going.

"You now stand to inherit my money instead of the company. You will do exactly what I tell you to do. The only difference is now you instead of waiting until I retire, you have to wait until I die."

He thought about this. £150M. That was better. She'd done what he'd planned to do anyway. But what if she lives another thirty years? But now he'd get the money and not have to bother with working. The trouble is he might not get the money for years. "What do you want me to do?"

Aunt Ruth stroked his cheek. "Why, Primrose. I still want you to become my pretty niece and now I have the time to turn you into a real girl."

Aunt Ruth's smile spread on one side of her face.

Chapter 6 – Relief

David sat on his bed, head down. His bedroom was decorated in pink. The walls were a light pink wallpaper covered with dolls and flowers. She'd provided him with a double bed but the covers were also pink with pictures of cartoon princesses and handsome princes covering it. It was a little girl's bedroom and he was a 35-year-old man. Underneath his short pink baby doll nightie and smooth shaved moisturised perfumed body.

Aunt Ruth sat close beside him, her hip against his, her hand on his bare thigh. His pink nightie hardly covered matching small pink panties that struggled to hold his penis and balls in. Her close proximity and hand on his smooth thigh a couple of inches from his genitals was making him semi-hard.

Aunt Ruth wanted a serious chat with him before he went to sleep. He wasn't tired, but 9.30 was bedtime. Aunt Ruth's rule. Did he still need to follow her rules? If he wanted £150M he did.

Aunt Ruth was still dressed in the business clothes she had worn for the afternoon Zoom board meeting. She wore a knee-length grey skirt, black stockings, four-inch heels and a crisp white blouse done up to her neck. Reading glasses hung from her neck on a thin silver chain. His aunt was always dressed well, even on a weekend evening. Her hair was as immaculate, as ever, she still wore her pearl ear studs in with a matching necklace.

He stared at the floor. This sixty-two-year-old woman looked younger than her years. Her perfect brown hair had to be dyed and her smooth face was no stranger to Botox, he was certain. Her makeup was professionally applied, her perfume expensive; it wafted deep into his nostrils.

Her older-woman sexiness, her assertive domineering persona, her clothing, his little baby doll nightie made his head swim. And his penis was now rock hard.

"I want to talk to you, Primrose," she said, leaning into him. Her perfume floated up his nostrils; it was musky, feminine and strong. "It's about your future. I'm going to do some things differently. Starting tonight."

David frowned, this type of thing usually meant trouble for him

Before he could ask, she continued. "Primrose, I don't like the idea of you having male thoughts. You need to be more like a girl."

What she wanted she couldn't always have. "What do you mean, Aunt Ruth?"

Her eyes moved down, towards his panties. He followed her eyes down, panic in his body. A lump poked out from below the hem of his nightie. He moved his hands down to cover the front of his panties.

"Were you going to play with yourself tonight? After I left?"

"No," he spluttered too quickly. This was exactly what he'd had planned.

Aunt Ruth shook her head. "Tut tut. This is what I meant by not wanting you to have male thoughts." She waved a slim hand. "Move your hands away, Petal."

He pushed his hands harder over his erection.

"Remove your panties, Princess, I want to see what you have down below and what I have to work with."

He moved away, horrified yet intrigued. "Aunt Ruth, you can't be serious." His face burned.

"Primrose, remove your panties. I want to inspect you. It's important to the changes I'm going to make now I have more time for your development. And I have something I need to do."

He opened and shut his mouth twice. She wanted to see his penis? His erect penis. Weird. Aunt Ruth was behaving oddly.

She leant across, pushed his hands away and pulled his panties to his knees with a swift yank. His erect penis shot into the warm air like a salute, the top of his nightie resting on the base. He gasped in humiliation.

Aunt Ruth raised her glasses to her nose and peered down at his erection. She grasped it halfway down between two fingers and pushed it to his body and inspected it. She ran her fingers through his pubic hair.

His eyes shot wide and he froze, his mouth dry. What should he do? As he remained in a stupor, Aunt Ruth checked his penis and balls. What had got into her?

She hummed softly and pulled on his balls to see them more clearly. "Good, good."

"What's good?" he squealed an octave higher than his normal voice.

She smiled. "It's good you're not very big down there. I didn't want you with a big willy and balls." She nodded. "It's small and feminine-like, even though it's very hard." She looked up at him and giggled like a little girl. "Naughty girl." She thought for a moment, holding his penis. "I don't like the word willy. It's kind of boyish and you're a girl. Now let me consider the options. We need a girly name for it." Aunt Ruth put two fingers to her chin.

David's throat closed up in humiliation. His Aunt Ruth was sitting next to him with her fingers around his erection. Ecstasy and horror in equal measures.

"Don't look so shocked, Primrose. You love it or you wouldn't be so hard, would you?" It wasn't a question. She rubbed a thumb along the hard shaft. She let go and sat up. "We'll call her Penny, what do you think?"

David screwed his face up. "You're going to call my willy, Penny?"

Aunt Ruth looked pleased. "Yes. Princess Penny." She rubbed a thumb over the end and giggled. "She's so cute. Small and hard." She looked serious. "We will need to trim your pubic hairs. Remove them from around Penny and her pussy balls and then shape a cute feminine triangle. She traced it out with a fingernail.

This was surreal. He understood his aunt wanted him feminised but here she was holding his penis, calling it Penny and talking of shaving his pubes. This was odd.

Ruth was deep in thought. "Wait here. I need to get some things."

She got up and left his bedroom. David looked down at his erection, the bare penis head peeking past the retracted foreskin, red and swollen. This was beyond weird. He pushed his erection back into his panties and waited for her to return.

A few minutes later Aunt Ruth strode back into the room. She held a box of tissues and a pair of blue latex gloves. She put the tissues on the bed and slapped on the gloves like a surgeon about to perform an operation. Now what was going on? Aunt Ruth was getting even weirder.

She looked up. Her brow creased. "Who told you to put Princess Penny away?"

David shook his head, *Princess Penny*? "Aunt Ruth. Come on," he spluttered.

She looked down on him, gloved hands on hips. "Get Penny out. Now. Primrose."

His erection hardened more at her words. She was referring to his penis as *Penny*. The past few months of his life had been the strangest ever. They were getting stranger.

"I'm waiting," she said.

His aunt's face reddened; he didn't see her mad often and didn't want to make things worse. Anyway, she had seen his erection now so, if it kept the peace, he could get it out again. His stomach turned and wobbled at the thought.

He closed his eyes, breathed in and pulled his panties to his ankles. He sat up and opened his eyes, looking down. His penis was firm, hard and red.

Aunt Ruth's face softened and she pushed her body into him as if to say *'we're two girls sharing secrets'*. The problem was, they were his secrets, not hers.

"Good girl." Aunt Ruth raised her hands like a surgeon about to operate and pulled her gloves tighter onto her hands.

What was she going to do next? He didn't have to wait long for an answer to his silent question.

"I want to remove your male urges." She screwed up her nose and threw her hair back with a shake of her head as if to get it out of the way.

She looked sexy. He wished she didn't, she was his deceased uncle's wife. She put her blue latex-covered gloved hand on his erection. She wrapped her fingers around it. "This isn't ideal, Primrose, but it will have to do for now until I've got things sorted." She snorted. "I don't want you playing with yourself in secret so this is temporary, you understand. Until I can figure out what to do with little Penny and her... Urges."

She rubbed her fist up and down his erection in a gentle movement, her eyes fixed on his hard penis.

"Aunt Ruth, what are you doing?" His voice came out high.

"I'm going to clean out your sissy juices." She pulled out several tissues with her other hand as she continued to rub up and down his erection. She passed him the tissues without breaking rhythm. "Take these for when Penny spits and make sure you catch it all. I don't like mess, especially sissy mess." She grimaced and shuddered.

He took the tissues in a daze. He tried to look away but all he could see was Aunt Ruth concentrating on rubbing his erection in her blue medical gloves. She wore a pained expression. This shouldn't be so nice; she was in her sixties and his uncle's wife.

It was too wonderful. He should complain, he should push her away but he couldn't, he was caught in a trance. He couldn't speak or move. A warm sensation rose through his body and up to his face. His balls ached, his erection throbbed. He watched as she concentrated with a faint grimace as she worked on his erection. She had one hand around his balls and the other worked up and down his shaft. She was gentle and careful.

"Let me know when you're about to squirt, Primrose, so we can point Penny at the tissue for you to capture the mess and clean up."

He came.

Chapter 7 – Consequences

Aunt Ruth moved to jump away. She was too late as a long thin line of his creamy cum spurted into the air. It hit her with a dull splat in the face. A streak of semen hung from below her left eye and across her cheek and mouth. A drip formed from her chin. Another burst of cum shot out before she had a chance to react. The spurt of light grey semen flopped down across her skirt like drips from a modern artist's brush swipes.

David's penis spasmed again; another spurt shot across her skirt and onto her shoes in a slow wide arc. David fell back. More globules of ejaculation oozed onto the bed covers from his withering penis.

The ejaculations finished and he sighed in deep satisfaction. That was incredible. His aunt had masturbated him. So wrong yet so great. The faint sound of a car travelling on the road outside and a bird in the garden were the only sounds. He settled into the bed in a soft woozy dream. Sheer ecstasy and release. Something was wrong.

He opened his eyes after several moments. Aunt Ruth held her hands out; her mouth caught in a silent scream. A drop of cum fell from her chin and plopped on her lap. She wiped the back of her hand across her face. She stood and held her skirt out, treading around his discharge on the floor. For a few moments, she remained mute and expressionless.

Then she looked at him. Her face creased hard. "I told you to aim at the tissue, selfish girl. Disgusting. Look at my skirt, my shoes. The floor."

She wiped her face again and inspected the cum clinging to the palm of her hand. She struggled to maintain her composure, flustered. David cowered into the bed.

"You will clear this mess up while I change and have a shower." She looked to her shoes. "Disgusting. Horrible. What was I thinking trying to help you? I can't trust you."

David stood up and sat back down, his eyes shot to the cum on the floor, her shoes, her clothes. "I'm sorry, forgive me." His eyes widened in horror at the long stringy damp patches of his discharge over the front of Aunt Ruth's skirt. "I'll clean..."

Her eyes narrowed. "Leave me alone, horrible selfish girl. I can see I'm going to have to consider another approach to curtail your nasty urges."

She stormed to the door and turned back, a long finger pointed at David. "I've indulged you for too long, girl. From now on, you're going to do everything I want. Everything. All I asked from you was to indulge me by being a well-behaved obedient prissy niece. Someone I could dress pretty. Someone I could have a girl's chat with. It's all I asked. I've tried to balance my wishes by not being too pushy but by guiding you. Nor did I go too fast, taking you on this journey carefully. And this is your selfish response." She scowled. "If you want to see a penny of my £150M you're going to be doing everything I tell you from now on."

She slammed the door behind her. The wall and door frame shook. This was not going to end well.

Chapter 8 – Chastity in Pink

David tottered along the pavement past the shop fronts, balancing on thin heels. Aunt Ruth held his hand, her face dispassionate and fixed. She was on a mission although he didn't yet know what the mission was. Whatever it was, his 'little incident' the other day was the cause. If she hadn't wanted him to make a mess, she shouldn't have masturbated him. She'd not taken it well when he'd shot onto her face and clothes. Accidents happen. Not for Aunt Ruth they don't.

His feet ached and his calves burned in the new six-inch heels. He wore a white chiffon dress that flicked around the top of his thighs. The breeze blew it, exposing the bottom of his bum cheeks and the small bulge in the G-string panties.

A wide pink ribbon hung from the back of his blond hair in a huge bow. He wore a pink leather collar on his neck, fixed with a small heart-shaped padlock. A thin golden chain about nine inches long ran between his ankles. Aunt Ruth had clipped it to his shoe buckles, restricting his steps. As if he could have managed more in these heels.

His eyes flicked everywhere. This was such as revealing and feminine outfit; he'd have been embarrassed wearing it if he'd been female, let alone a male. It was something a little girl would wear. Except for the high heels.

He drew looks from everyone. "Head up and be proud, Primrose. You're a girl, a selfish girl it's true, but pretty all the same." Aunt Ruth continued to look ahead, fixed on the day's mission. Whatever that was. "If you don't walk like a prissy girl, I won't be holding your hand next time, I'll be holding a leash attached to your collar. Wiggle your bum like a sexy girl." A grin flashed on her lips. He didn't like the new Aunt Ruth so much. She was harder. Bitter at the 'incident'.

He pulled his head up and blinked behind one-inch long black false eyelashes. Aunt Ruth had ramped up his feminisation, putting him in ever more revealing, submissive and girly clothes. Punishment or part of his ongoing increase in feminisation? He wasn't sure but he didn't want to annoy her by asking.

She had forbidden him to cum since the 'incident'. She said she was going to do something more permanent about it. She didn't trust him. She kept him in sight, watching him when he went to the toilet and making him sleep on a blow-up bed in her bedroom. She didn't want him touching himself and making another 'mess' when he was out of sight, she'd told him. She'd made it clear today's trip to the shopping centre today was to fix what she called his control problem. Following the 'incident'.

Aunt Ruth led him into a side road off the High Street. It took them down a hill making walking even more challenging. His toes crunched into the front of his high narrow shoes. He was sure he'd have blisters later. David shortened his steps in an attempt not to fall forward.

The area became rougher, the road was lined with charity shops, betting shops and boarded-up windows. Posters were pasted to walls and windows. Small posters covered the lampposts advertising massages with photos of buxom young ladies. It was not the typical district he'd have imagined his aunt would go to.

Aunt Ruth stopped at the foot of the hill. They stood outside a plain shop front with a blank frosted glass window. A large ripped poster advertised a pub band. A sign on the solid wooden door to the side door read, *Over 18s only*. Above the door, a larger sign read, *Private Shop*.

Aunt Ruth pushed the door and strode in pulling him with her. The door opened into a large well-lit rectangular room lined with a sales desk at the far end. A hand-written sign on a piece of paper taped to the back of the door read, *facemasks must be worn in the shop*.

White metal shelves stacked with items lined the walls. Other stand-alone shelves in the same style were staggered through the shop. Harsh fluorescent strips glared from rectangular ceiling diffusers.

David scanned the metal shelves: dildos, butt plugs, sexy maid and lingerie clothing, paddles and whips, rows of DVDs and magazines with semi-naked people and women with giant boobs on the covers. Boxes of blow-up dolls called Letitia and Roxy laid stacked against one wall.

A young man in a cheap blue suit browsed the magazines. An older gentleman with balding grey hair and a beer belly inspected the cock cages. Both of them wore blue medical face masks; they turned to look at David as they walked in. The men's eyes were on stalks.

"Their fantasy has walked in, Primrose dearie," said Aunt Ruth. "I bet they don't realise you have a little something extra down below. Or maybe they do?"

Aunt Ruth seemed to have calmed down now they'd reached their destination. David would have preferred her to have remained angry with him than her teasing him.

She pulled David's hand towards the sales clerk, standing behind a counter. She was a stocky attractive woman of around forty with thick black hair and strong red lipstick. She watched David approach with an air of amusement; she had spotted him as a male. She pointed to another sign on the counter — *face masks must be worn inside the shop*. David and Ruth attached their masks from under their chins.

The clerk wore a tight white blouse; the front buttons were undone halfway exposing her cleavage and large mounds of spilling breasts. He guessed, by her faint smile, she had seen it all before and his appearance was not unusual in the shop. Her eyes flitted down to the hint of a bulge in his exposed panties peeking from under his tiny dress. Her eyes lingered there for a few moments. Her eyebrows raised a fraction before looking back up to his face and to Aunt Ruth.

"I'm looking for a male chastity device for Primrose," Aunt Ruth announced in a voice several notches too loud for David's comfort.

From the corner of his eye, he saw the middle-aged man's head shoot up from studying a pink cock cage to gape at him. The shop clerk's eyes creased in delight.

"I want something comfortable for her," said Aunt Ruth. "Do you do a fitting service?"

The lady walked from behind the counter. "Yes, we do."

This sounded like another humiliation to David. His shoulders sagged. Mind you, the shop clerk wasn't bad. Matching her skin-tight blouse, the sales lady wore a short skin-tight mid-thigh black pencil skirt. It was several inches shorter than David would have expected on a mature lady. It outlined her large firm bum and muscular thighs. It strained against her thighs as she strutted towards them. The lady oozed a powerful sexual assertiveness. She had chosen her vocation in sex-associated work well.

"Our Spectre XR range comes in various sizes. This is a good choice for her."

She marched to a shelf and picked up a rectangular box. She returned to where Aunt Ruth and David stood. He tried to not stare at her firm, large breasts bursting from her blouse. The photo on the side of the box showed a white cage in what appeared to be plastic. The thin bars mimicked the distinctive penis shape.

The shop lady undid the top of the box and took the cage out, wrapped in clear plastic. She took it out of the plastic and passed it to Aunt Ruth. Aunt Ruth turned it over in her hand. She lifted it twice in her palm to gauge its lightness. She looked satisfied with the result. A small integrated lock was located on the top; three tiny keys hung from one of the bars.

"This is our bestseller," said the clerk. "It comes in five lengths and has seven different ring diameters to attach around sissy balls of all sizes. You can mix and match." Amusement glinted from her eyes. "It's made from lightweight tough nylon. It's very solid and perfect for long term use as it's so open and light." She grinned mischievously. "And of course, you can see their little cuties all tucked away inside." She hunched her shoulders as if to indicate how sweet this was.

"Aunt Ruth, I don't want..." David's voice switched to a hush. "My willy locked away. I promise not to play with it."

Aunt Ruth looked up from the cage. "Shut up, Primrose, it's not up to you. And don't be silly, you're a sissy girl, you don't have a willy." His voice was far too loud for David' comfort again.

The shop clerk's eyes widened. "That told you, Primrose." She looked back at Aunt Ruth. "You can't trust sissies. They love to play with their little cuties. It's always the best strategy to lock them up."

David looked away only to see the two men gawping at them. Their heads shot away to pretend to inspect sex toys.

"Yes, that was the problem." Aunt Ruth said. "She was unable to control herself; she came everywhere. It was disgusting. You should have seen the mess." She shook her head. "On second thoughts, you shouldn't."

The shop lady sniggered and then pulled a serious face. "If you buy the Spectre XR device today, there's a 50% discount on the Spectre Butt Plug range." She walked to the shelf below the cock cage shelf and took a similar box. She turned. "These are excellent. Five different shaped and sized anal plugs in black silicone."

She returned and showed Aunt Ruth the cover. Aunt Ruth scanned it with interest.

"They are soft and comfortable, according to my husband, "said the clerk. "And perfect for daily use." She removed the clear plastic bag containing five soft devices. "They are great for closing up her little booty during the day. You can also use them to loosen and stretch her in preparation for anal intercourse." She looked at David. "Sissies need to be penetrated. I can peg my husband with an eight-inch dildo. Although I also stretched him out with an anal stretcher."

"That doesn't sound too good," said David.

"Shush, Primrose," said Aunt Ruth, glaring at him. She looked away. "Do carry on; ignore her."

"Yes, of course, madam." said the shop clerk. "I imagine you'll want her playing with other sissies. I like to do this with hubby. It's important to get their little booties bigger and become accustomed to having things inserted there. This might be butt plugs, dildos, or sissy erections. And real men. Or maybe you would want to peg her with a strap-on?"

Aunt Ruth gasped and put a hand to her mouth. "Goodness me, no. I'm not going to partake in any kind of sexual activity with Primrose; she's my niece. But I'll take them as I like the idea of blocking her little hole up." She lowered her voice conspiratorially. "And to stretch her and get her ready for sissy friends. Or even male boyfriends."

"Aunt Ruth," said David. "I don't want a boyfriend."

Aunt Ruth put the cock cage on the counter and her hands on her hips, looking at him through lowered eyelashes. "I told you, Primrose-Petal, it's not up to you. I want you to live as a sissy girl and this means having sissy friends. Friends to love." She shook her head at the shop clerk. "She can be such hard work at times."

"I imagine, madam. Sissies always are. They're so needy." The shop clerk said. She put out an arm to indicate the back of the shop where a dark curtain was drawn. "Would you like to come to the fitting room? We can measure Primrose for her chastity device."

David stepped back, his attempts restricted by the ankle chain.

The clerk continued. "And, if you wish, madam, we can have an inspection to see what butt plug size would be most suitable too."

David gasped in. "Inspection?" Things were getting worse.

"Yes," said Aunt Ruth. "This sounds perfect." She turned to David. "Shall we follow the nice lady to the fitting room?"

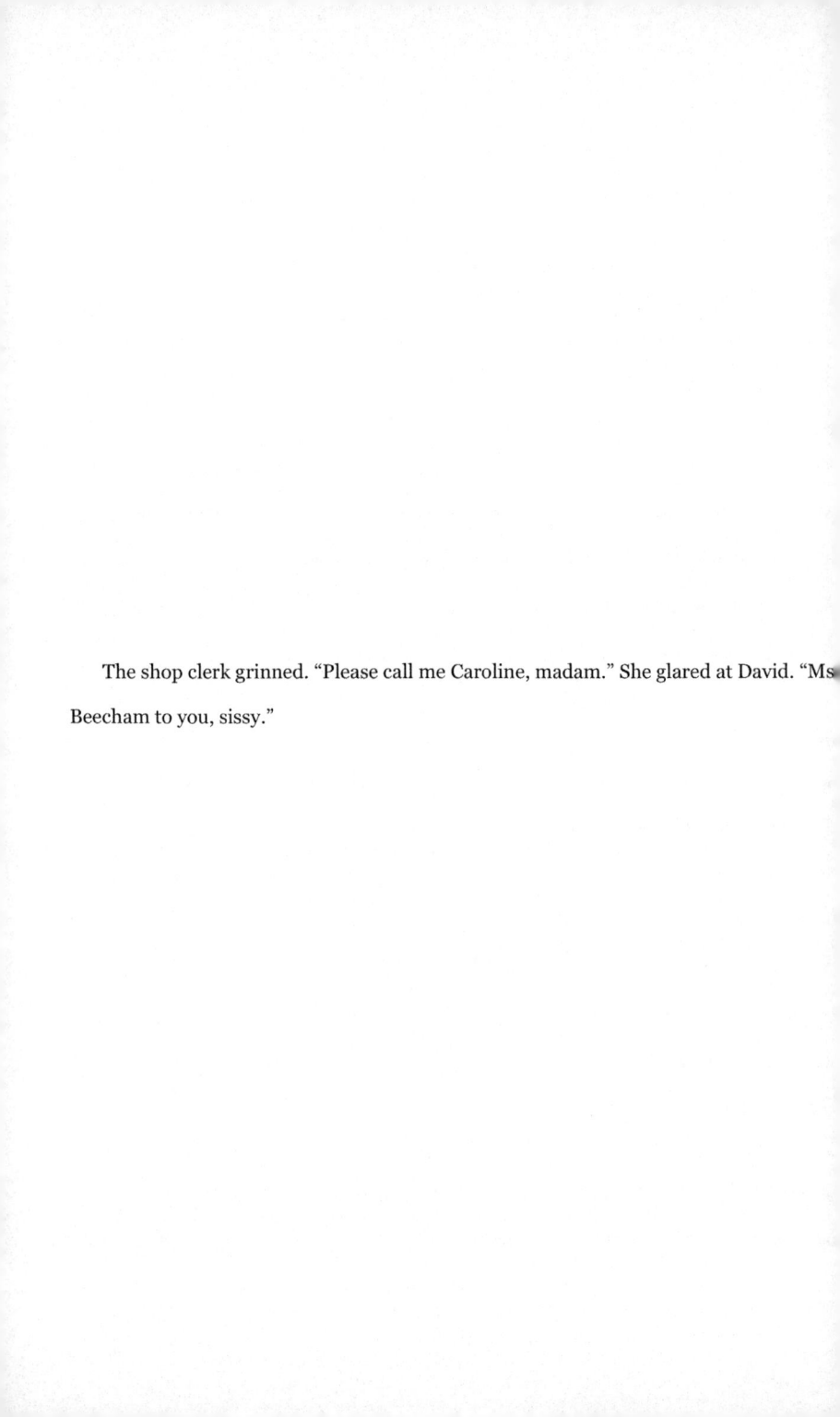

The shop clerk grinned. "Please call me Caroline, madam." She glared at David. "Ms Beecham to you, sissy."

Chapter 9 – Locked and Unloaded

The backroom doubled as a store. Cardboard boxes lay around the walls and a small square table sat in the middle. The shop clerk put her hand on the back of David's head and pushed down against the tabletop. He was bent over the table, bare bum in the air. Caroline pressed against the flange of a butt plug lodged inside his bum. She wore white latex medical gloves; a box sat on a side table with a glove half hanging out. A small box of tissues and a tub of wet wipes lay next to the gloves. David's chiffon dress hung over a chair in the corner, his panties hung around his locked ankles.

"It's not comfortable, auntie" he squealed.

"Do be quiet, Primrose," said Aunt Ruth.

"Primrose is tight but after regular use, the butt plugs will loosen her up," said Caroline. "Or you can think about the anal stretcher if you want to open her up? She'll be ready for sissy clitties in no time. Or a real man's cock."

"That would be marvellous, Caroline," said Aunt Ruth. "I can imagine either scenario in the future."

David attempted to lift his head, Caroline held it down hard. "No," he said.

"I want you, as my pretty niece, to entertain suitable partners. It's part of your development."

"What partners, Aunt Ruth, what are you talking about?"

Aunt Ruth sighed long and hard and shook her head. "Caroline. Let's measure up for the chastity cage."

Caroline lifted her hand away from the back of David's head and peeled off her latex gloves. She dropped them in a waste bin. He stood up stiffly. Caroline put a hand to her mouth and giggled, her shoulders hunched in amusement. His penis was rock hard.

"I can't measure it when it's hard," she said. "We need her soft and the only way is to make her cum of course."

"What?" said David, thinking it might not be so bad. Humiliating yes.

"You don't have much of a vocabulary, do you?" said Aunt Ruth. She leant to the small table and pulled out two fresh latex gloves from the box. She slapped them on her hands.

"Aunt Ruth? You're not?"

Caroline passed her a handful of tissues which Aunt Ruth cupped around the end of his erection. She grabbed his penis and rubbed. "This will be your last time so make the most of it."

Last time? Waves of guilty pleasure flowed over him casting the question away.

He saw Caroline watching with detached fascination as Aunt Ruth's latex-covered hand rubbed his hard penis. Despite the lack of sexual affection and the sensation this was like milking a cow's udder for Aunt Ruth, it was exhilarating. He couldn't comprehend why but allowed himself to enjoy every moment. It wasn't as if he could do anything about it now Aunt Ruth had made the decision.

Caroline creased her eyes in a cute smile at him. That was the final touch of humiliation he loved. He shot into the tissue, an explosion of cum. He gasped in intense pleasure. At least he hadn't cum on Aunt Ruth's face and clothes this time. Maybe she'd forgive him seeing he had controlled himself better this time? He pulsed twice more and leant back in relief against the table. Caroline passed Aunt Ruth two wet wipes.

Aunt Ruth tossed the cum-filled tissue into the waste bin and took the wet wipes. She cleaned away the remaining drips around the head of his shrinking penis with a grimace. She threw the wipes in the bin too. She stripped off her gloves.

"I'll get the tape measure," said Caroline. She went through the curtain and into the shop. David heard her telling a customer she would be another five minutes as she was doing a chastity cage fitting on a sissy. David cringed.

She returned with a yellow cloth tape measure. "Here we go," she said cheerfully, as if measuring up the flaccid penis of someone who had just ejaculated at the back of her shop was an everyday occurrence. When he thought about it, it probably was a regular task in her line of work.

Caroline pushed the metal end of the tape under and onto the base of David's penis and the coolness made him squirm. She ran the tape along the length to the tip. She leant in close to read the size. Her warm breath fell on the slightly exposed tip and a quiver skipped through his stomach. More of this and he'd grow hard again.

Caroline screwed her eyes up to focus. Two and three-quarter inches. "Small," she said. She looped the tape around the middle of his penis and leant in again, more warm breath and David felt a stirring.

"Just under three inches girth. Not large," Caroline announced too loudly for David's comfort. He was aware of the customers waiting on the other side of the curtain.

He looked to the curtain and was horrified to see Caroline hadn't pulled it back properly after returning. He saw the back of a man in a suit on the other side of the counter. "You haven't pulled the curtain properly. Someone might see us," he said.

"Don't worry about the curtain, Primrose, let Caroline do her job and measure little Penny Princess."

Caroline knelt on her haunches. David watched her tight skirt ride up and her powerful thighs and squash against her calves. She ran the tape measure around the base of his balls and penis. "Small sissy balls too," she said. "I can see why you've become a sissy."

The young man at the counter spun round. His eyes dropped to the sight of Caroline with a tape around David's balls. His face seemed to melt as his eyes turned into circles.

Caroline stood. "I suggest the Spectre XR model B. It's usually best to have the cage half an inch smaller for a better fit. Any smaller you run the risk of reducing the clitty size over time."

"Really?" said Aunt Ruth, her interest piqued..

"I don't want that," said David.

"Oh do be quiet, Primrose." She turned to Caroline. "Put the smaller one on her. A smaller clitty sounds perfect. It will be a much cuter Penny Princess if smaller."

Caroline went back out into the shop. David wanted to complain but bit it back when Aunt Ruth raised a finger in his face. He closed his mouth. Caroline returned with the Spectre XR box with size A written on the side and the length: 1.5 inches. His penis would be squeezed up tight in this caged prison.

Caroline took the cage out and clipped it around his penis, squeezing it in as if pushing washing into a washing-machine drum. She clicked the integrated lock shut with a small key. She passed the keys to Aunt Ruth. She popped them into her handbag. David squirmed and tried to readjust the cage. His penis was squashed.

The two ladies looked at David's penis crammed into the tiny cage. Aunt Polly touched it. "I'm considering not allowing her to cum again, Caroline. What do you think?"

David's mouth dropped open. Where did that idea come from? "What do you mean, Auntie? How can I not cum again?"

Caroline looked down at his caged penis. "In my experience, madam, chastity is beneficial for sissies. It makes them more submissive and feminine. And there's no mess of course. I keep my husband locked. Unless he's playing with other sissies, of course. And he's not my husband any more. More of a housewife stroke housemaid."

Polly pondered this for a moment. "No, I didn't mean chastity. I want Primrose to have sissy friends or boyfriends. I don't like the idea of her making a nasty mess after what happened the other day."

Caroline touched Polly's arm. "However you achieve it, it's a very sensible approach to not allow her to ejaculate." She sniggered. "Besides, think of the fun you can have teasing her."

David did not like the way this discussion was going. "You can't be serious, Auntie?"

"Put your clothes on, Primrose and cover caged Penny Princess up." Aunt Ruth passed him his dress.

He dressed in a sulk and they went back out into the shop. Five customers milled in the room and the man still waited by the counter. He eyed David up and down twice. It was a look of envy.

Caroline took a paper bag from under the counter and put the butt plug box and empty Spectre XR box into it. She lifted up another cage and held it out for Aunt Ruth to see. It was pink nylon without any cage area, just a flat piece of plastic with a hole where the penis shape should have been.

"After your comment about making her little cutie smaller, I thought you might like to see this too?" Caroline opened the device and closed it again. The man at the counter followed every movement with fascination.

"Once she's got used to the current cage and she's reduced in size by half an inch or so, you might want to move on to this one. It would squish her cutie down in size to practically nothing."

"No, Aunt Ruth, no," groaned David.

Aunt Ruth tapped his cheek in a slight slap. "Don't Aunt Ruth me, Primrose." She shook her head at Caroline. "Thank you, I'll take that too. I like the idea of Penny Princess becoming smaller and more feminine. It will become a pretty little nub of a clitty. That sounds perfect."

Caroline put the mini cage into the box and popped it into the bag. She rang up the total on the till and pushed forward the card reader.

David leant in to whisper into Aunt Ruth's ear. "I still have the butt plug in, I need to go to the backroom to take it out. It's a bit sore."

Aunt Ruth tapped her credit card on the card reader and typed her PIN. "No, Primrose, you'll leave the butt plug where it is. We're stretching you, remember?" She sighed long and her voice bounced around the shop. The other customers looked their way.

Aunt Ruth took David's hand. "Thank you, Caroline." She pulled David to the shop door as the customers watched them leave in stunned silence.

Chapter 10 – Reunion

David pulled off the pink medical face covering as he left the shop. He looked down at the pavement in despair. He wasn't looking and bumped into someone. He looked up to see a slim young lady with tumbling blond hair and massive boobs an inch from his face.

David faced enormous boobs held in beneath a low-cut elasticated white top that seemed to have been sprayed on. The boobs were almost falling out from a visible bra. His eyes dropped to her long thin legs and tiny excuse of a pink ra-ra skirt. He may have been feminised but a girl in a skimpy outfit and big tits drew his attention every time.

"Ouch, my arm." The woman put a hand over the top of her left arm, long red nails dug in. She breathed through clenched teeth, in pain. Tears twinkled in her heavily made-up eyes.

"I hardly touched you," said David, a moment of anger flashed at her exaggeration.

"She had her second COVID vaccination this morning. Her arm is sore," said an older woman standing next to the blond girl.

David looked up into the blond girl's face for a moment. The girl batted her long black false eyelashes, a smile grew across her wide red lips. He knew her from somewhere.

"Hello, Amy," said the blond girl looking a little happier and still holding her upper arm.

It couldn't be, could it? Was it Polly?

Before he could answer, the older woman next to the blond girl spoke. "Why, if it isn't Amy the *boychik*."

He looked at the middle-aged woman. "Ms Lipman?"

"You know these two people?" said Aunt Ruth, an amused tone in her voice.

David looked back and forth between Ms Lipman and Polly. "Yes, Aunt Ruth. Ms Lipman was my mistress before I ran away to live with you. I guess she'll be pissed off with me." He moved behind Aunt Ruth for a semblance of safety, putting his hands on her shoulders.

Ms Lipman leant in and ran her fingers down David's face over Aunt Ruth's shoulder. "Amy, you are a silly *boychik*. I'm not a prison warden, I did what you wanted deep inside. You were always free to leave. And you did, although it might have been polite to say goodbye beforehand."

People began stopping to gape at the two well-dressed middle-aged women with younger girls dressed as bimbos. Ruth was alert to the growing interest.

"Ms Lipman, how nice to meet you. I'm Ruth Amey. Let's go somewhere less open, I'm sure we have a lot to discuss. We have this pretty thing in common." She looked around the street. And spotted a coffee shop back towards the High Street. "There." She pointed. "I'll buy coffee and we can have a nice chat about Primrose. Or is that Amy?"

"You're Amy's relative?" Ms Lipman pondered the information for a moment.

Ruth nodded slowly. "Her aunt."

"Her aunt, well I never." Ms Lipman thought about it. "Anyway, I was going to buy a new chastity device and a bigger butt plug for Polly but there's no rush. Let's have coffee and have a talk about the sissies."

David watched the two ladies with mounting horror. This was what he did not want: Ms Lipman and Ruth getting to know each other. Ms Lipman was full of bad ideas when it came to feminisation. The group set off towards the cafe.

They went in and the two ladies sat in the window. They sent David and Polly to buy the drinks. An astonished young man served them; his eyes roved over Polly's low-cut top.

The two sissies returned with the coffees on two trays and sat together opposite the two ladies. David didn't like the way Ms Lipman and Aunt Ruth were laughing together. They were getting on well and that would be bad news.

"I hear you're now called Primrose," said Ms Lipman. "I suppose Amy Amey didn't work." She looked up in thought. "Primrose," she said rolling it around her mouth as if savouring the flavour. "I love it, so feminine. A pretty flower like you."

She tweaked David's face with two fingers as if he were a child.

"And Louise has told me how you and Polly became such intimate friends when you lived there," said Aunt Ruth. "I'd love to have seen that little show. You didn't mention that to me, Primrose, you naughty girl."

David looked away, his face burning red. Memories of the night he'd sucked on Polly's large erection flashed in his mind. Ms Lipman and the two young female police officers had cheered and laughed. He shuddered at the thought of the taste of Polly's cum in his mouth; the bitterness on his tongue and in his throat.

"I've invited them round for dinner this weekend." Aunt Ruth's voice broke through his nightmares.

David found himself breathing too fast, his head felt light. He didn't want Ms Lipman giving Aunt Ruth any more bad ideas beyond the ones she already had.

"And I accepted," said Ms Lipman. "Ruth and I have so much in common and I have some ideas for her. It will be wonderful. I'm so looking forward to it."

David gulped again. "Wonderful ideas?" His worst fears were coming true.

"Yes," said Aunt Ruth. "You and Polly will serve us. I hadn't thought of that." She looked for a moment at her new friend, Ms Lipman, then back to David. "Louise will bring the pretty pink housemaid dress you left at her place. It sounds divine." Her face beamed at the thought.

This couldn't get any worse, he thought.

"And they will be staying the night so you and Polly," she said, her eyes darting between the two sissies. "Will have the chance to become well-acquainted again."

David and Polly looked at each other. David's mouth dropped open. The hint of a smile appeared on Polly's lips.

Chapter 11 – The Mistress Dinner Party Affair

Saturday evening came too quickly for David. Aunt Ruth and Ms Lipman had exchanged phone numbers at the café and spoken a couple of times to make their plans.

Ms Lipman and Aunt Ruth sat together in the dining room; David and Polly worked in the kitchen finishing the dinner. Polly was a trained cook and David was the helper. He peeled potatoes and prepared the vegetables. He didn't have a clue how to cook.

Ms Lipman had dressed the two sissies identically; Ms Lipman had made good on her promise to bring the pink satin maid dress he'd left at her place. Ms Lipman had said a sissy uniform was always a good idea and it was cute to dress sissies identically.

Their dresses were short and flared from high waists below their chests. Stiff white petticoats held the flares out. They wore tiny white aprons with frills around the edges. The aprons were too small to be anything other than decoration.

David found it difficult to work in the six-inch heels; Polly had less trouble. Black suspender straps held up their fish-net stockings. The stocking tops and suspender straps showed.

Once they had prepared dinner, the two sissies brought it to the dining area where Aunt Ruth and Ms Lipman sat. They wore formal dresses.

Aunt Ruth wore a fifties-style white dress with black polka dots. It fell an inch or two below her knee. She wore a wide black belt that showcased her slim waist. Her sleeveless dress highlighted well-toned arms. She'd brushed her dark straight brown hair back in her distinctive style. Long earrings hung from her small neat earlobes. David felt a pang of lust for her. He told himself not to be ridiculous, she was more than twenty years older than him. And she was his aunt. Sort of. It seemed wrong to lust after her.

Ms Lipman's body shape was bigger and curvier. Her dark dress clung tight to her body, following the lines of her shape.

The dining room was less a corporate meeting room now Aunt Ruth had sold the company. The walls were now in a light green shade and the fresh paint smell lingered. The painters had worn face masks throughout the work last week, Aunt Ruth had insisted on it. Several old-style paintings hung around the room. The pictures were scenes of the countryside with thatched cottages, horses and carts full of hay in sunlit fields.

Aunt Ruth had persuaded Ms Lipman the two sissies could have dinner at the table with them. Ms Lipman had initially wanted them to eat in the kitchen. Ms Lipman told them to eat in silence and follow orders without comment. Dinner passed without any humiliating incident for David.

After the sissies cleared up the table, the ladies retired to the living room. Aunt Ruth told the sissies to join them there once they had finished working in the kitchen.

They finished their work and David and Polly wandered into the large living room at the front of the house. David's calves ached from working and walking in six-inch heels. The balls of his feet hurt because of the pressure of walking on tip-toes. He wondered how Polly could be so light on his feet in the same style of shoes.

Aunt Ruth and Ms Lipman were sitting on the four-seater sofa as they came in. David and Polly stood waiting for instructions. David guessed Ms Lipman would have something embarrassing for them.

He thought again about the humiliating evening when he was living at Ms Lipman's home. He remembered Polly's little something extra beneath her skirt. And then Ms Lipman made him suck on Polly's *little something extra* that wasn't so little at all. And swallowing Polly's cum; in front of Ms Lipman and the two pretty police officers. Ms Lipman had forced him. What could he have done? He'd had no choice, it wasn't as if he wanted to suck a penis. No. One thought kept coming back to him. It hadn't been the worst thing ever. He brushed the thought away and shuddered. Those thoughts were wrong.

Heavy red velvet curtains were pulled shut over the long windows at the front of the room. In one corner, a dark grand piano loomed, its lid propped up. Often, Aunt Ruth relaxed by playing classical songs and Beatles' tunes. David preferred the happy Beatles music over the complicated classical music. Classical seemed to have no obvious tunes to him.

Behind the piano, a floor to ceiling bookcase covered the wall. It was crammed with books, from business titles to novels. He never understood why people read books; they were so boring; there were no pictures. TV was so much better. Or comics. And if you wanted to find out something important like what *the 10 cutest cats* looked like or *the biggest ever tits*, you looked it up on YouTube. Books? No thanks.

Several books on the shelves were by Lady Alexa. He recalled this was the same author he'd seen on that man's shelves, the one who'd bought the company. They had strange titles such as *Feminized and Pretty, A Sissy Cuckold Husband* and *Maid To Serve*. What the hell was a *cuckold*? A kind of bird? David thought that *made* was spelt *m a d e* but he wasn't sure. He'd try to remember it was *maid* but he'd probably forget.

Ms Lipman and Aunt Ruth were in a deep whispering conversation. This had to be bad. Aunt Ruth looked up. "Sissies, we want you to hold hands."

David sighed. He guessed they would want him to do something like that but holding hands wasn't so bad. At least it wasn't sucking on Polly's erection. They clasped each other's hands, interlocking fingers. Polly's palm was cool.

Aunt Ruth pointed a slim black remote control and pressed it. Slow soft music sounded out from small speakers near the piano. Horrible, that classical stuff. She put the control down on a glass coffee table and picked up a glass with ice cubes and a large slug of tan liquid.

"We'd like you to slow dance together, sissies," Ms Lipman said.

"What?" said David.

"I don't like the word, *what*," said Aunt Ruth. "It's *uncouth*. You will say, *excuse me Mistress and curtsey*."

Aunt Ruth was generally pleasant to him, now he was feminised, but her face now looked as if a dark cloud had fallen over it. He did not know what *uncouth* meant but he had upset her. He didn't want that.

He dropped Polly's hand and dipped a curtsey holding the hem of his maid dress. "Excuse me, Mistress." He felt the ring of his chastity cage dig into his balls. It reminded him it had been some time since he'd cum and he could do with being able to masturbate.

"I said we want you to dance to the music, together. You have to put your arms around each other and touch cheeks together. Like loving girlfriends."

David wanted to say *what* again. *You must be joking* was the expression he also wanted to use. He held his tongue and turned to Polly. Polly looked down at her toes then up at him, batting her eyelashes. She didn't appear worried, the opposite if he had read her face correctly. Polly put his arms around David's waist and moved in close, pressing his body against David's. Polly pressed a cheek against David's. His perfume was strong. Polly's thighs moved against his, their cages touched. This was far too close.

"Primrose." Aunt Ruth's voice cut through the light piano music.

David put his arms around Polly. Their chastity cages clicked together through their panties.

"Stop." Ms Lipman stood. She glided up towards them. She stooped in front of Polly and pulled his panties to his knees. She pressed a small key into the cage lock on the top of the device and let it fall into her hands.

Polly's enormous penis fell out from below his short dress. David watched in horror as it expanded like an inflating sausage-shaped balloon. It became rock hard in a second. David gasped in astonishment. He remembered having that in his mouth at Ms Lipman's place and shuddered. He was unsure if it was horror or a weird desire. How could a slim feminine sissy like Polly have a penis so big?

Ms Lipman moved her hands to David's chastity cage. She unclipped it and his penis fell free. She looked at it for a few moments with a smirk. He was far smaller than Polly. Worse still, it hardened too. It had to be due to the length of time Aunt Ruth had kept him in chastity. That was a normal reaction to Aunt Ruth keeping him restricted for so long, he told himself.

"Primrose has a cute little clitty," she said and stood up.

David was now rock-hard. It had to be the length of time he'd not cum. It had to be that, he couldn't be so excited by Polly. Could he?

Ms Lipman returned to sit next to Aunt Ruth. The playlist flipped onto another track, a seventies slow dance by a long-forgotten band. At least it was better than the dirge that had been on before.

"Dance, sissies." Ms Lipman swirled a hand in the air.

David looked down at his erection sticking out at right angles below his dress and pointing at Polly. Polly's erection pointed back.

"But Mistress, our willies will touch if we get close." His eyes were stuck on the two erections.

Ms Lipman smirked. "Stop delaying, sissy. That's the idea."

Chapter 12 — The Breast of Friends

Gentle music floated through David's woozy brain. He tried to concentrate on this rather than Polly's eight-inches of steel-like penis pressing up against his stomach.

Polly's erection twitched; Polly was excited by their slow dancing. David couldn't decide what he thought although his own penis had made up its mind.

Ms Lipman manoeuvred them to a spot in front of her and Aunt Ruth sitting on the sofa. David and Polly's bodies locked together as they swayed side to side, moving round in slow circles.

"Closer, get in tighter," said Ms Lipman. "Put a hand under each others hair and stroke your necks."

Polly pressed in harder, his penis denting further into David's stomach.

"You're going to be girlfriends and fall in love. I'm so happy for you both," said Ms Lipman.

David's body stiffened. Polly was uncomfortably feminine and sexy, despite the solid erection. His huge breasts pushed into David's chest. It was a contradiction, a puzzle. Feminine and masculine. Huge tits and a penis.

"Faces together, girls, cuddle like you mean it." Ms Lipman was in her element giving orders.

Aunt Polly sat forward. "I wanted my niece to meet someone nice. I was thinking of a handsome young man but Polly seems to be the best of both worlds." She sniggered, a finger to her lips. "Maybe this is an easier transition for Primrose?"

Ms Lipman nodded in agreement. "*Boychiks*, like Polly, are so submissive and compliant. It's the best first step for your niece. Once she's got used to Polly, she can move on to a nice young man."

Aunt Ruth looked at Polly wistfully. "Where did Polly get those wonderful breasts from, Louise?"

David wanted to ask the same question. They were pressed up against his flat chest and helping to distract him from the feeling of a massive erection pressed against him.

"I have a friend who's a successful plastic surgeon," said Ms Lipman. "She gave Polly implants. And the cute round bum." She turned to Polly. "Stop for a minute and remove your dress and bra so Ruth can see what a great job Dr Simmons did with you."

Polly blinked once and turned her back to David. "Be a sweetie and unzip me." He put a hand on one hip and turned his back. He threw David a glance over a shoulder.

David stared for a moment. Aunt Ruth nodded at him to get on with it. David pulled on the zipper on Polly's dress and took it down to the end point above Polly's bum. Polly's body was sculptured like a girl's, a tiny waist, curvy hips and a bum that curved out.

Polly shuffled his shoulders out of the dress. It fell to the floor in a pile. He stepped out of it and turned back to face David, a pout on his lips, eyes wide. Polly wore a black low-cut bra that pushed up his enormous breasts. He now wore only black six-inch heels and fishnet stockings. The suspender belt was tight around his small waist, two straps clipped to her stocking tops framed a giant straining erection.

Polly wriggled his hips twice, making his erection waggle. He giggled and looked at his bra straps. Polly slipped one arm, then the other, out of the bra straps. He pulled the cups down to reveal two wonderful mountainous breasts. His nipples were large and erect, the areola wide like small red saucers. David slavered without realising.

Polly twisted the bra around and unclipped it. He let it drop to the floor, wriggled her chest at David and turned to face Aunt Ruth.

Aunt Ruth's eyes popped at the sight of Polly's gigantic breasts. They were out of proportion to Polly's slim frame.

"I went for a 40DD size," said Ms Lipman. "A top-heavy look helps to emphasise a sissy's femininity." She wiggled a finger, calling Polly to her. When Polly got to her, Ms Lipman lifted up one boob. A narrow scar ran under her mound. "This is where the implant goes in. Then once it heals, you can hardly see anything. The breast falls down over and covers the scars."

It was unusual to see Aunt Ruth stuck for words. She soon recovered. "How do I go about getting these for my niece?"

David stepped back at the thought of having breasts. His erection hardened. "No."

The women ignored him. "I'll give you my friend's details. Dr Elizabeth Simmons. She's one of the best. Not cheap. Of course. But the end results are worth it if you want Primrose looking good." She ran a hand over Polly's curvaceous hips and pert bottom. "And Elizabeth is the best surgeon around at giving new girls these sexy bums. Primrose will need this too otherwise she will always be a man in girl's clothes."

Aunt Ruth sat on the edge of her seat. David was cursing inside at Ms Lipman. She had enthused his aunt beyond anything he'd expected. This was getting worse.

Ms Lipman clapped her hands. "Anyway, back to the present." She stood up. "Girls. You're to become loving girlfriends so you need to show more affection. Tonight is sissy love night."

Polly moved back towards David, a look of tenderness on his face. Polly's erection pointed at him like a guided missile.

Chapter 13 — It Must Be Love, Love, Love

"Lips together, sissy-girls." Ms Lipman waited expectantly. Aunt Ruth sat in stunned silence, disbelieving. "I want to see nice big wet loving kisses."

David was looking away when Polly planted his lips onto him. He turned his head to one side, Polly's lips smeared saliva across his face. David screwed up his face and wiped away the saliva with the back of his hand. Polly may look like a sexy bimbo girl. But she was a he and David didn't kiss males, even if they had big tits. Especially one with a cock that big.

Ms Lipman stood up more quickly than David expected and took his head in both hands. "Primrose, you will kiss pretty Polly and you will enjoy it." She folded her arms. She meant business.

David felt his bottom lip quiver. "Aunt Ruth, tell Ms Lipman that you don't want me kissing males."

"I will not, young lady." Aunt Ruth glared at him. "If you're to stand any chance of your inheritance, you will become the niece I always wanted. That's not too much to ask for in return for £150M, is it?" She sat back. "But you're free to do as you please, Primrose. It means I'll remove you from the inheritance, of course."

Was money more important than kissing a man? Was Polly a man any more? More female than male, apart from that huge penis. He turned to face Polly. Polly blinked and widened his eyes.

David had to do this. He puckered his lips and moved towards Polly. Their lips glanced together. Polly's lips were soft, warm, his breath minty. Polly opened his mouth wider, his tongue touched against David's lips then onto his teeth.

"Nice and wide, girls, and let me see those tongues pushed deep into each other's mouths. This should be love." Ms Lipman stood close, David smelled the brandy on her breath. Polly's breath was more enticing.

Polly pushed his tongue in deep. He lashed it around David's mouth, stroking his teeth and wiping over the roof of his mouth. David pushed his tongue into Polly's mouth and moaned in pleasure. They pressed their lips harder, their teeth clicked, their tongues danced together like snakes to a charmer's tune. David panicked. He was enjoying this.

Ms Lipman guided the two sissies to the sofa. Aunt Ruth got up and the sissies sat, their mouths locked together, sliding, kissing. David caught the sight of Polly's erection straining up, a small drop of pre-cum oozing from the tip. David's penis was also rock hard and pointing up from under his dress.

"Now, pretty sissies," Ms Lipman said. "Put your hands around each other's clitties." She bent down and took David's hand. She placed it around Polly's raging penis. She moved it up and down to show him what she wanted. The warmth of Polly's hard erection flowed through his hand like an electric current. His fingers caught the dripping pre-cum; it squished between his fingers.

Ms Lipman took her hand away from David's. David rubbed his hand up and down Polly's erection. His thumb rolled over a single soft large vein and he squeezed against it. Their kissing intensified, their saliva mixed, their tongues jousted.

Polly took David's penis and David sighed as it slipped into Polly's mouth. He hadn't cum for a long time and this was all he wanted. The chance for release, to explode and find ecstasy. Polly ran his fingers over the end of David's penis; David gasped again. He shouldn't be liking this but he needed it. The release was not far away; it bubbled in his balls and tingled in his stomach. He looked up into Aunt Ruth's eyes. They were unblinking, full of fascination.

"Don't rub too fast, girls, I don't want you cumming everywhere. Not yet anyway." Ms Lipman's voice was stern.

David didn't want to stop but his release was delayed for now. But she'd said, *not yet*. That meant soon.

"Louise." Aunt Ruth's voice was cool. David didn't like it when she used that voice, it meant she was not pleased about something. His fears were confirmed. "I don't permit Primrose to cum. It's such a nasty sticky mess." She shook her head and shuddered.

Louise touched Aunt Ruth's arm. "She's your niece, you can do as you please with her, but why would you prefer she doesn't cum? Aren't you enjoying their love?"

"I adore it. It's what I want to see. Let them continue." Aunt Ruth bit her lip. "But." Aunt Ruth hesitated at a memory. "Primrose came all over me once when I was trying to help her. She made a terrible mess and I had to throw my skirt away as the stains were too deep. I even found some in my hair. After that little episode, I made a rule that she was not to cum any more." Her eyes locked with David's. "It's for the best after what she did. She showed she was selfish. She has to pay the consequences for her selfishness."

"Disgusting, Ruth. These sissies are so selfish." Ms Lipman glared at David. "Did I tell you about Primrose? When she lived with Fiona Ryder, the author, she came all over my shoes." Ms Lipman's hand remained on Aunt Ruth's arm. "To be honest, I thought it was funny as I saw that she was a born sissy. But I understand you completely. Sissies struggle to control themselves so we have to do it for them. Don't worry, we won't allow her to ejaculate if that's your rule."

Ms Lipman removed her hand from Auth Ruth's. "Polly, make sure you don't let Primrose cum. If she gets over-excited, stop until she calms down." She smiled at Ruth. "What do you think?"

"That sounds perfect, Louise."

That did not sound perfect at all, thought David. The idea of two women watching him have sex with another male was not his idea of fun. At least he'd get a moment of pleasure. Aunt Ruth was snatching that away. He wanted to cum. He was going to cum. His balls ached, his penis throbbed, his head hurt with the need. There was no way she could stop him.

"Primrose, sit up straight," snapped Ms Lipman. "Polly, on the floor and between Primrose's legs."

The two sissies jumped to their positions. "What now, Mistress?" asked David, sulking after his aunt told everyone he wasn't allowed to cum. Well, he was going to cum and they wouldn't be able to stop him. He'd plead an accident, he couldn't help it. She'd restricted him for ages, what did they expect? It was unfair. Yes, this was it. He was going to cum. A smirk fell over his face.

"Polly," said Ms Lipman.

Polly looked up from between David's legs.

"Be a good sissy and suck on Primrose's clitty."

"It's called Penny," said Aunt Ruth.

Ms Lipman clapped. "Oh, I love that. How cute. *Penny.*"

That was too much. David stood up. Ms Lipman pushed him back down again. "You're girlfriends, you have to love each other. Now sit back and let Polly show you her love."

Polly's long blond hair dragged over David's thigh. A swish of heavenly lightness against his delicate skin. Polly pecked a small kiss on the end of David's erect penis. David shivered in delight. If this continued, ejaculation would be close.

"No," said David in a weak half-hearted voice. He didn't want Polly to stop at all, he wanted to maintain a reluctant aspect. It was time to cum whoever was making it happen. Polly wasn't the ugliest girl he'd had sex with. Even if Polly wasn't actually a girl.

David laid back; Polly's tongue flashed against the slit on the end of his penis. Polly's warm breath swarmed around the exposed swollen end of his erection like soft velvet. His soft lips wrapped around it, his mouth descended over the entire length. The tenderness and having his penis inside a smooth mouth made David swoon. Polly's mouth moved faster and faster, up and down his erect shaft, up and down. Polly moved faster as David's erection swelled further than he thought possible. So good. Polly's tongue licked around the end as his lips moved up and down like a warm ring of soft fur.

Polly's hands wrapped around David's balls, his fingers squeezing in time with the sucking. They kneaded into David's ball sack, almost uncomfortable but not quite. Enough to feel. Polly was an expert. Up and down, up and down. Ecstasy surged in David's brain like a sudden drug infusion.

David opened his eyes for a moment to see the blond mane of hair over his penis. Moving, swirling around his erection. He closed his eyes tight and screwed them up waiting for the volcanic explosion of cum to erupt into Polly's mouth. It was going to happen. It bubbled in anticipation, a boiling stew of desire.

Here it comes. Release. Relief. David swooned in a trance. Euphoria was imminent, his juices stirred around his balls, his insides, his erection. He was going to beat Aunt Ruth's stupid rule. He was going to cum and it was to be an explosive triumphant release after so many weeks bottled up. He was going to cum. Now.

Chapter 14 – Cum Again

The warmth around his erection vanished at the point of ejaculation. A chill hit his exposed penis head. David whipped open his eyes. Polly was sitting back on his legs, head down, eyes peering up, lips pursed provocatively.

Polly licked her lips. If only that tongue was on his erection, he'd shoot a jet of cum into that sexy mouth. David's tense erection twitched. No lick came. One more touch and the dam would break, the dyke collapse, the walls would come tumbling down. No lick came.

David glared at Polly. He didn't care if Polly was a male under that hair and those massive tits. He wanted Polly to finish what he'd started. David swung to look at Aunt Ruth and then Ms Lipman. Both sat impassively. He stared back at his erection as it throbbed swollen and red. Polly watched him with his mouth open showing the tops of his teeth. His tongue wiped around his lips again. How David needed that tongue on his penis.

"Why?" gasped David. "Why did you stop? I was about to cum."

"I know," said Polly, his lips pursed, he batted his eyes.

"I need to cum."

"I know," said Polly. "I wasn't allowed to make you cum. Otherwise, I would have. Like last time."

David sat forward, anger burning in his face, his erection so hard and desperate it ached. "I need to cum."

Polly raised his hands to say it's not my fault. David grabbed his erection and pulled on his foreskin. If Polly wasn't going to help, he'd damn well do it himself.

Someone whipped his hand away. Aunt Ruth stood over him. She brushed a hand through her hair. It remained in shape.

"I know you want to cum, Petal." Aunt Ruth's voice was soft and concern glinted in her creased eyes. "But you have to realise and remember." She waited, standing over him.

"Remember what, Aunt Polly?"

She shook her head. "That you mustn't cum, Petal." Aunt Ruth kept hold of his hand and stroked the back of it with her other hand, trying to soothe him.

David opened his mouth and shut it again as he tried to clear his mind from the desperation. She was being kind to him and not at the same time. It was as if she thought that not allowing him to cum was helping him somehow. She thought she was.

"I could cum in Polly's mouth and she could swallow it and it would keep everything clean and not be messy." He looked down. "I know you don't like the mess, Auntie. I'm trying to come up with other ideas." *Come* didn't seem a good word in the circumstances.

Aunt Ruth stroked his face. "I know, Princess, but I have a solution and I made a decision. That's how it is. I'm not going to change my mind on this one." She shook her head again. "No, you made that nasty mess once. I can't risk that happening again." She shuddered theatrically and raised her eyes to the ceiling at Ms Lipman. "No, this is for the best, Princess."

Aunt Ruth sat next to David. "We'll let Princess Penny calm down then you can start again, getting to know Polly better." She nodded to his erection and kissed him on the cheek. "You'll see that you can live without ejaculations once you become accustomed to it. It'll take a little time but eventually you'll stop thinking about making a mess."

They waited for a few moments and David's ardour reduced. Aunt Ruth was right, things did calm down. His erection fell flat.

Ms Lipman jumped up once she saw he'd calmed. "Excellent." She pointed at Polly. "Back to work on Primrose."

Polly slid between David's legs again and grabbed his flaccid penis. Polly began sucking on it. It became erect again.

Ms Lipman stood over them. "Slowly, Polly, get her nice and hard. No more. I want to see you make love next. Like lovers do."

David didn't like the sound of that. What did she have in mind? For now, he laid back and enjoyed Polly's soft gentle lips worked up and down his erection. It was better to enjoy the moment.

"Enough." Ms Lipman pulled Polly away.

She took Polly's hand and pulled him up and to the dining room table. She bent him face-first over the table and ripped down his panties. She spread his legs wide. Polly's bum was fuller and rounder than his slim frame suggested it should have been. It was like two large melons. Ms Lipman slapped one of his bum cheeks once.

Aunt Ruth sauntered over, her eyes on Polly's bum. "How on Earth did she get such a pert rounded bum?"

Ms Lipman smirked. "Dr Elizabeth Simmonds. You need her number, Ruth."

Ms Lipman raised an index finger at David and wagged it towards her. Now what was she going to do? David stood up and walked awkwardly towards Polly. David's erection led the way, his embarrassment at the situation undimmed. He stopped behind Polly, his small dress draped over his exposed erection.

Ms Lipman put both hands on Polly's exposed bottom and pulled her cheeks apart. A large open anus faced David. "In you go, lover girl." She turned to Polly. "I used an anus stretcher on her daily until she got big enough to take any size. Many sissies and men have been up there. You'll find her big and she'll take your little thing with no problem."

David didn't understand what she wanted. Surely she didn't mean she wanted him to put his penis in Polly's bum. Ms Lipman pressed a hand on the small of David's back and the other hand on his erection. She guided it to the entrance to Polly's waiting hole. His question was answered.

David pushed back against Ms Lipman's hand. "No, you can't be serious? You want me to put my penis in Polly's bum?"

Aunt Ruth put her lips to his ear. "No Primrose, we want you to put Penny Princess in there. We want to see you two making beautiful love together." She stood straight, her hands went to her hips. "If you two are to become lovers, you have to make love." She stared. "Now."

David's erection suddenly felt freezing cold. Ms Lipman continued to squirt cold gel over the end from a tube labelled with a K and something else. She wiped it around the end with the palms of her hands and pushed him to Polly. The end of his erection slipped into Polly's hole without resistance. David whined in surprise: Polly's feminine bum swallowed up his entire erection.

"Good girl," said Ms Lipman. "Now all the way to the end."

Not waiting for the shocked David to react, she pushed hard against the small of his back. He slipped it all the way in, slapping the top of his legs against Polly's bum cheeks. David grunted in surprise and Polly let out a satisfied, '*oh*'. Polly was smooth and soft inside, not what he'd expected. Not unpleasant and not unlike that of a girl's vagina, although the last time he'd done this with a girl was a long time ago. It had been that Eastern European health worker with the peroxide hair. Why was she on his mind?

"Er. You're supposed to be making love to your new lover, Primrose. Polly is waiting for you to show her some love. So are we."

David stayed in the same position.

"In and out, make love," said Ms Lipman.

She grabbed either side of his waist from behind and guided him. He moved with her pushes. He pulled outwards, leaving his penis head just inside Polly. He then thrust back all the way in. He thought he could feel something against the end of his penis. Polly murmured again when the tip touched it. He pushed in hard; Polly moaned in pleasure again.

This was weird. Aunt Ruth and Ms Lipman were standing back with their arms folded. He withdrew and pushed in. David grabbed Polly's hips and withdrew then pushed in again. Polly said, yes. David closed his eyes. This was good. Like being with a real girl.

He moved in and out rhythmically. It was better than good. It was wonderful. In and out, Polly's bum moved side to side and towards him in rhythm to his thrusts. Who would have thought this was as good as doing it with a girl? But his penis was inside a man's bum. Sort of.

For a moment David froze. No, this was not good. He was having penetrative sex with a man. This was all wrong. A slap rocked the back of his head.

"Get on with it."

He pushed in again and closed his eyes. A thought came to him. Another chance to cum? Polly might not realise this time; his penis was inside Polly's bum, not his mouth. David relaxed and thrust in and out, in and out. This time, he'd cum and no one would realise. He dropped his head back and went faster. He breathed loudly through his open mouth. The warm feelings of imminent ejaculation flowed up through his stomach and into his erection. Ha. He'd fooled Aunt Ruth this time.

A tug on his waist and his erection fell from Polly's bum and waved in the cool air.

"Not so fast, Primrose." Ms Lipman had her arm around his waist. She looked down at his throbbing member. "Not there yet but we can't take any chances. Ruth's rule, remember?"

Polly stood up and turned around. Aunt Ruth took David by the arm and led him back to the sofa and sat him down. She looked down at his erection. "Primrose isn't yet ready. Be a good girl, Polly, and rub her with your pretty fingers to get her to the point."

Get him to the point? It would be cruel if she didn't let him go all the way. Polly sat back between David's legs and took his erection in one hand. Polly's breath was warm on the end but it was his hand doing the work. The fingers worked up and down his erection with a practised smooth style. This felt great; David sat back. What were they doing to him, teasing and playing? They were going to let him cum this time. Why else did Aunt Ruth tell Polly to rub him? Finally, he would get to cum. She wasn't that cruel. Was she?

Polly worked his fingers on his straining penis; so good, so loving. Polly ran a forefinger over the slit on the end, playing with the lubrication of the pre-cum as it oozed out. He wiped a fingertip around the base of his penis head. Soon it would be an explosion of real cum.

Polly used his lubricated fingers to work at David's erection. Their eyes locked. Polly was pretty, his hair peroxided and styled. His false eyelashes and slim face were cute. His bright red lips were thick, luscious and ripe for kissing. Yet, something male remained. David couldn't put his finger on what, some residue of a past masculinity. The facial structure beneath the make-up and the plucked eyebrows, false eyelashes and thickened lips?

Polly's fingers flowed over his penis and around his balls then up the end, fingertips tracing patterns on the exposed head. It didn't matter, this was good.

David arched his back as the feelings of ejaculation surged in him. Slow and soft, Polly's fingers worked on his erection, fingernails scratching lightly. David's penis hardened and the feelings of release built. Any moment, he'd blast his load.

Polly leapt onto the sofa next to him and planted his lips on David's. They locked hard, tongues exploring each other's mouths. Polly grasped his erection and wrapped his entire hand around it. He pumped it, faster and faster, his fist beating down on the top of his balls. He pulled hard on David's erection, stretching, holding for a moment before pushing down again.

It was so good, so erotic; they kissed with a passion David had never experienced before. Not even with Olga had been this good. The Ukrainian health worker. Or had she been Bulgarian? It didn't matter, this was better. Polly closed his eyes, not like Olga, she had kept them open staring into space. Or was she called Nadya?

Who cared if Ms Lipman was watching, who cared if Aunt Ruth was laughing at him? This feeling was real, exciting, intoxicating. Their mouths smeared around each other's faces. Their tongues left trains of saliva smeared over their cheeks. All the time, Polly rubbed his hand down David's penis, harder and faster on his penis. David arched his back again; he moaned a throaty groan of pleasure. Here it came, redemption. Finally. An exhilaration and frenzy of emotion soon to explode into the best orgasm ever. He was on the cusp, the point of explosion was tantalisingly close. One more tiny rub from Polly's expert fingers and he'd reach the point of no return. There would be no stopping this.

Polly stopped kissing, his hand fell away. David screamed in despair.

Aunt Ruth stood over him, a single finger held out wagging at him. "Now, now, Primrose. You know the rules. No cumming."

Chapter 15 — Satisfying Polly

David's penis burned. It stung. It was as if several weeks' of semen was locked up in his penis and balls but a lock gate closed at the last microsecond. The pressure pushed hard. He grimaced in agony. His erection was bursting at the seams. He sat forward, his head down.

"Forget about Penny for once and concentrate on Polly." Ms Lipman stood over David. "If you're going to love Polly, you will need to focus on her needs too, Primrose. You're being selfish, thinking only about your orgasm and forgetting your beautiful girlfriend."

Words wouldn't come into David's brain, it was fogged with desperation. Polly wasn't his *girlfriend*. What was Ms Lipman on about? Polly moved close to David. Polly's massive erection pointed at his face, an inch from his lips. Surely not? Polly's expression was demure, there was a longing in his eyes. Polly was pretty, in an exaggerated way.

"Open wide, Primrose," said Aunt Ruth. "Polly gave you a loving blowjob so you should reciprocate. Come on, don't be selfish."

Polly pressed his large hard penis head against David's closed lips. A moistness touched his lips and a salty musky smell lifted into his nostrils. Disappointment shit into Polly's eyes. David kept his mouth closed.

David licked his lips involuntarily to remove the slimy pre-cum. Polly slipped his erection in and onto David's tongue. A taste of sour salty milk hit David's tongue for a moment then the texture of firm smooth skin.

Polly pushed his hand through David's hair, around his ear. His gentle fingertips massaged his temple. David relaxed and Polly's erect penis slid all the way into his mouth. It was like a warm sausage. A giant sausage.

Polly moved his hips back and his erection slid back, rubbing on the top of David's tongue. Polly moved forward and David felt Polly's rolled-back foreskin and smooth penis against the roof of his mouth and tongue. Intoxicating sensations.

Polly pushed his other hand through David's hair and ruffled it lovingly. David's erection stiffened further. His erection tingled as if sparked with electricity but the urge to cum had receded. It wasn't far off though.

"Lips around Polly's pretty clitty, Primrose." It was Ms Lipman.

David closed his lips around Polly's penis. The memories of what was going to happen shot into his mind. He'd had to suck off Polly once before. His first ever blowjob. He remembered the slimy warm cum shooting into his mouth. Warm then cool after a few instants: slimy and salty. He shuddered and took Polly's erection in one hand. At least there seemed to be a no cumming rule this time. He shuddered again at the memory of swallowing what had seemed like a never-ending ejection of slimy warm cum. The last time this had happened.

David moved his mouth up and down Polly's enormous hard shaft. He went down as far as possible and pulled back to the end and rubbed his tongue over the hard penis end. He went back down, feeling the large penis head against the back of his throat before moving back. Up and down. At least this wasn't as messy as licking a woman. Or as smelly. His Ukrainian girlfriend had been particularly wet down there, smearing his face when he licked her out. Or was she Russian?

Polly moved his hips with the movement of David's mouth along the erection. Polly moaned and threw his head back. His long waist-length peroxide blond hair tossed about like a wave in a wild tempest. Polly's eyes rolled up beneath his false black eyelashes, his mouth open a little, a gasp escaped.

David's hand went to his own erection but Ms Lipman pulled it away. "Concentrate on Polly's pleasure. Don't be so selfish."

David pushed his mouth up and down on Polly's shaft. It must have been eight or nine inches long, it filled his mouth. How could such a slight person have such a massive cock?

Polly's penis stiffened in his mouth and Polly gasped again. Uh oh, Polly was about to cum. David pulled away and sat back, leaving a straining, hard erection throbbing inches from his mouth. Polly opened his eyes in surprise.

"What are you doing, Primrose?" said Aunt Ruth from next to him.

"I stopped, she was about to cum."

Aunt Ruth sniffed out. "And?"

"I thought we weren't allowed to cum. You don't like the mess and the smell."

Aunt Ruth looked to the ceiling. "You are not allowed to cum, Primrose. Polly is."

That wasn't fair. "But what about the smell and the mess?" David asked desperately, trying to avoid having to swallow Polly's slimy cum.

"It's easy. You'll take it all in your mouth, swallow it, and lick Polly's clitty clean."

"But why couldn't Polly do this to me?"

"Because you're not allowed to cum, Primrose."

"I don't understand."

"I know." Aunt Ruth was becoming annoyed.

"Explain why Polly can cum and I can't, Aunt Ruth."

"Because that's my rule, Primrose. Now get on with it. Polly deserves her orgasm." Aunt Polly's voice rose.

"And I don't deserve it?"

"No."

David saw he wasn't going to win this debate. He moved back to Polly's waiting, straining erection. He put his lips around it and closed his eyes. It wasn't so bad to have Polly's penis in his mouth. It was... satisfying? No, it was more: it was erotic, exciting. He wasn't about to tell Aunt Ruth that snippet.

Polly's erection immediately stiffened, it was solid. David moved his mouth and lips up and down the erection, Polly gyrated his hips, groaning. He was back into the groove. Polly moved faster, he was pushing his erection faster and faster into David's mouth, rubbing his hands through David's hair. Groaning and moaning in a trance.

A shot of cum hit David's tonsils like a liquid bullet. Polly's erection jerked and he pushed his erection in further and back inside David's mouth. David swallowed the first load, it flowed down his throat like a line of oysters. He cringed at the warm, salty and slimy goo in his throat, mouth and tubes. Polly's cum was filling him up. He choked for an instant at the volume pulsing from Polly's penis, it wasn't ending. He took a breath through his nose then swallowed another load, then another. Would Polly ever stop?

Polly slowed, breathing fast. David swallowed one more time, catching his breath. Polly stopped pulsing cum into David's mouth. The shrinking penis oozed a little more cum, then a little more. David sucked on it and swallowed again. Warm and oozy. He had got a little more used to it. Not so bad.

No more seemed to come out. David fell back on the sofa, his eyes closed, gasping through his open mouth. Two pairs of hands began to clap. "Good girls."

He opened his eyes. Ms Lipman and Aunt Ruth were beaming. Polly sat down next to David, kissed him lightly on the lips, laid a hand across his thigh and flopped. No one spoke for several minutes.

Aunt Ruth got up and called Ms Lipman to the other side of the room. They whispered for a few minutes then returned to the sofa.

"OK, show over for tonight." Aunt Ruth clipped the cock cage around David's now flaccid penis. "We don't want you getting any ideas and besides, we've agreed Polly will move in with us. Polly will be sleeping with you now we've seen how you love being with each other so. And we wouldn't want any accidents, would we."

Chapter 16 — What's the Story Morning Glory?

David walked into the kitchen and was surprised to see a man having coffee with Aunt Ruth. Polly was still asleep upstairs in their bed. Their bed?

"This is George."

George was ogling David and Aunt Polly seemed comfortable with this reaction. David wore a short pink dress that flared from the waist with short sleeves. David thought it might have suited a five-year-old girl going to a party but was less attractive on a thirty-four-year-old male. Aunt Polly thought otherwise.

"George, this is Primrose, my niece," said Aunt Ruth. "I'm sure you two will get along very well."

George was around 6ft 2ins tall. He seemed the same age as Aunt Ruth. His hair was silver and parted to one side. He wore an open-necked blue striped shirt and sharply creased dark blue chinos with shiny black shoes. It was as if he had tried to look casual but failed. His eyes glinted in restrained amusement at David in the little girl's party dress.

"Primrose is my sole living relative. When I die she'll get all this." Aunt Ruth swept a hand around the room and pointed vaguely to the back garden. "But I don't intend to go anywhere yet."

She giggled girlishly. That wasn't like Aunt Ruth at all. What was going on? The answer came.

"Primrose, I thought it was time I introduced my boyfriend to you."

David swallowed hard. George's deep blue eyes bore into him. "So," started George in a deep voice. "Primrose here." George pointed at David. "Pretty little thing, isn't she."

Aunt Ruth smiled in satisfaction.

"But." George's eyes bored deeper. "Is she totally a Primrose? If you know what I mean, Ruthy dear?"

David didn't like the way this was going and wanted to leave the room. At that moment, Polly walked in. Polly's hair swished around her; a mop of big peroxided hair with a large pink ribbon tied in the back. Whereas Aunt Ruth loved to put David in little girl's clothes, Ms Lipman preferred Polly to look as bimbo as possible. Ms Lipman always considered one had to 'over-egg' the style when the base material was male. Aunt Ruth agreed but preferred the little girl style. It was as if she was making up for a lost period.

George's eyes nearly popped out on stalks at the sight of Polly. David was thankful Polly had arrived and taken the heat off him.

"Well, well, what do we have here?" he said. His tongue ran around the top of his lips.

Polly curtsied awkwardly to George. He responded with a grin the size of the English Channel showing teeth that had seen hours of orthodontist work. His eyes flowed over Polly's outsized tits and long, almost skinny legs. Polly stood and tugged on her microscopic pencil skirt. It had ridden up in the curtsey revealing skimpy white panties. A huge bulge showed; the outsides of a pair of testicles flowed out either side of the thin cotton.

"Primrose and Polly are girlfriends. They live together here," said Aunt Ruth with what appeared to be pride. "They are in love."

"I'll bet they are." George's face smeared into a leer. David did not like this look one bit and he hoped not to be left alone with George. He cringed at the thought of George's wandering hands. George did not appear put off in seeing the two 'girls' were not what they appeared at first glance.

"They can hardly keep their hands off each other," said Aunt Polly. Not the response David was expecting or hoping to hear from her.

"I bet they can't," said George, his leer widening.

As if to demonstrate the point Aunt Ruth had made, Polly put his arm around David and kissed him full on the mouth. Polly pulled away, "Morning lover."

David went bright crimson. It had been a week since the 'event' with Polly in Aunt Ruth's living room with Ms Lipman. Polly had moved into his bedroom and shared his bed. Sure they'd kissed. David knew it was wrong, but Polly's giant tits were too much to resist so sure, he'd played with them. Kissed his nipples.

It was frustrating his penis remained locked away in a cage although he enjoyed Polly playing with his balls. That was better than nothing. But lovers? No. The temptation was there, nothing more. OK, Polly's penis wasn't locked away. It would have been churlish to not touch it for Polly. Selfish is what Aunt Ruth would have said if he hadn't touched it.

George was pleased at what he saw. "Don't mind me, girls, if you want to make out, be my guest."

David backed towards the door. "No thanks, George. We're fine."

"I don't know," said Aunt Ruth. "You seem a little flustered this morning Polly:"

Polly dipped a curtsey exposing her bulging panties again. "Thank you, madam. It has been a frustrating time, madam."

Aunt Ruth looked perturbed. "Oh no, why is that, Polly. I thought you loved living here with Primrose."

Polly looked downcast and to the floor. "I do, Madam, I do. But Primrose's clitty has been locked away for over a week and, and. I thought. You know."

Aunt Ruth walked to Polly and put an arm around him. "It's OK, Polly. You can tell me. What's the problem? What would you like?"

Tears welled in Polly's eyes. "We're supposed to be girlfriends but with Primrose's clitty locked away, we can't make love like lovers should. I want to feel Primrose in me, I want to feel her love. Physically."

Polly's tears fell stronger. David was horrified and backed towards the door.

"Don't mind me, girls. Do what you have to do." George's eyes glistened.

Aunt Ruth stroked Polly's head. "Shhh, Polly, that's alright. You know I can't unlock Primrose when I'm not around to keep an eye on her."

Polly sobbed. "Yes, I understand, Madam. Of course I do. But...But."

"But what, dearie?" said Aunt Ruth.

"I want to feel her in me. It's been over a week since that wonderful evening when I realised I love Primrose."

"What?" said David.

Aunt Ruth looked over at George. "Are you sure you don't mind? Polly's very upset and she needs to know she's loved. You don't mind if I let them do it?"

"Not at all, Ruthy. Let them bang away as much as they please."

"Thank you, George. I know it's a little unusual but you can't always plan things, sometimes nature has to have its way. You're so understanding." She turned to David. "Kiss Polly and show her some love; I'm going to get the gel and the key to your cage."

The situation had fallen apart in a matter of minutes. Did Aunt Ruth expect him to make love to Polly in front of this man he'd only just met? Or anyone? He had little more chance to think about it as Polly threw himself on David. His mouth covered David's, his tongue pushing around the crevices of his teeth and over his tongue.

Aunt Ruth returned and lifted David's dress. She pulled down his panties which fell to his ankles. She unclipped his cage. It fell away with a sense of great relief. To his horror, his penis shot to attention.

"Not too big down there is he? She?" said George.

"No our Primrose is not well endowed. We call it *Penny*, it seems more appropriate in the circumstances," said Aunt Ruth.

George nodded gravely. Aunt Ruth spun David around and undid the zip at the rear. His little dress fell around his ankles. He stepped out of it conscious of George's attention.

Aunt Ruth smeared gel over the end of his erection and slid back his foreskin with her bare hands. My, that felt good; the cool of the gel and the softness of his aunt's fingers. She guided him towards Polly. To his horror, he saw Polly was waiting, standing and bent at the waist. His skirt was squashed up around his waist like the belt it seemed to be. Polly's bare bum faced David, his bum hole large, open and distressingly inviting. Inviting? What had happened to him?

Aunt Ruth guided David into Polly's waiting hole. David's penis slipped all the way in, the end touching again at something soft. This felt wrong but wonderful. David looked up and saw George watching with rapt attention.

"Don't mind me, Primrose." George flashed a cheesy smile.

David had to ignore this and get on with things. If only he could do this in private with Polly, it would be better. But Aunt Ruth kept him locked, he had to make love with Polly with her watching.

David moved his erection in and out of Polly, gentle and loving. It was the only sex he was going to get so he may as well make the most of it. This time he'd disguise his oncoming orgasm. He would feign indifference and fool Aunt Ruth. He would use this opportunity to cum. Yes, he'd do this. George would see everything but more fool him.

"I love you, Primrose," said Polly.

David stopped for a moment. "What?"

"I love you."

David stopped moving, his erection halfway in Polly's bum.

Aunt Ruth whacked the back of his head. "Tell her you love her too." She turned to George. "Primrose can be such a selfish pain in the arse at times."

Ruth's face filled David's vision. "Now," she said, making him jump. She was annoyed again and he didn't want that.

If that made his aunt happy, what did it matter if he said it? "I love you too, Polly."

Aunt Ruth relaxed and moved away. David moved his erection in and out, deep and almost all the way out, then he thrust back in. The inside of Polly was warm and welcoming, smooth and sensual. A balminess filled David as he thrust into Polly, a feeling of caring and well-being. This was so good. The familiar feelings of cumming stirred in him. Keep calm, he told himself, don't give Aunt Ruth any clues about what's brewing in his balls.

He pushed a little faster, Polly groaned. David's hands were on Polly's hips, Polly moved slowly a soft grind. They moved together in harmony. So good. David closed his eyes, his face flushed warm. He imagined the semen flowing from his balls and prostate gland, gushing from both areas and meeting somewhere inside before edging towards his rock-hard penis. The semen entered his shaft and moved up inexorably. It was happening.

A hand pulled him sharply away. His erection throbbed in the air. One more tiny thrust and the seminal fluid would burst and blast out from the end and explode into Polly. One more touch. One more thrust, one more anything. Nothing.

"Primrose, Petal. That was a close call. Did you get carried away?" Aunt Ruth's hands remained around his waist. She seemed to think he'd forgotten he wasn't supposed to cum and it was a case of getting caught up in the moment.

David gasped in utter frustration. "Auntie?" If a feather or a mere draught of wind were to touch his raw, super-sensitive erection, he would have showered his fluids everywhere. No touch was going to arrive.

"Oh so cruel, Ruthy." George chuckled. "Primrose was about to shoot her load."

David spluttered and cawed. He screwed his face up. He was on the precipice, a touch away. Almost but it wasn't going to happen. A catch came to his throat.

"It's not cruel, George," said Aunt Ruth. "Primrose understands."

She stroked his head. David seethed in desperation.

Chapter 17 — The Future's Bright, The Future's Pink

"Primrose knows she mustn't cum. I stopped all her doing her messy business some time ago. She gets a little carried away at times. She'll be fine, won't you, Petal darling?" Aunt Ruth fluffed David's hair as she spoke to George.

No, he wasn't alright. He wanted to cum.

"Isn't it dangerous?" George looked concerned. "I wouldn't like you to stop me cumming."

"There's no danger of that happening, Georgie," laughed Aunt Ruth. "Anyway, it's not dangerous. In fact, it's good for her. Her sperms get expelled other ways in the body so there is no danger. And I read it increases stamina and thickens hair; that would be nice. She can make love to Polly more often. And have prettier hair. All this without her nasty sticky mess. Primrose is a girl now and I don't want to see her ejaculating like a boy."

They waited for David's erection to go down and Aunt Ruth clipped his cage back on. David ground on his teeth. He wondered if he'd crack them. "So you don't like George's cum, Auntie?"

"Don't be disgusting, Primrose. Anyway, that's different. George is a man and my boyfriend."

"But what about me?"

His question bored Aunt Ruth; her eyes looked to the heavens. "One day, when I pass on," said Aunt Ruth to George. "Primrose will get her inheritance of £150M as my sole living relative. In the meantime, I'm going to enjoy having a pretty niece. And pretty nieces have sissy girlfriends. And pretty nieces do not ejaculate like a boy, do they, Primrose? And of course, Primrose is free to leave any time."

David's mind raced. That was the point. Aunt Ruth had hit the nail on the head. It was as if this was decision time. Aunt Ruth had never forced him to stay. If he'd left, she would have let him. There'd be no inheritance, but this was no prison either. He saw Polly watching him. Polly was sexy, far sexier than the Bulgarian or Latvian health worker who'd given him a rash. Twice. Anyway, what did he have before all this? He'd lived in a one-bed flat in a poor district of London with no money. And a rash.

He picked up the little pink party dress. "No Auntie, your pretty niece does not ejaculate like a boy." It might be nice though, he thought.

"Excellent, Primrose" said Aunt Polly. "Because I made an appointment for you with Dr Elizabeth Simmons to see about a few changes."

THE END
OF
LOCKDOWN FEMINIZATION 3

I always like to hear from my readers so if you have any comments on the story or things you'd like to read, please drop me a line at ladyalexa@mail.com.

I reply to every one who writes to me because I love to hear from my readers.

If you enjoyed this story, please leave me a review. It really helps. Thank you.

Lady Alexa

xxx

Other titles by Lady Alexa

The Mother-In-Law Dilemma

Forced Feminization 1 — 7 Tales of Feminization

Forced Feminization 2 — 7 More Tales of Forced Feminization

Lockdown Feminization 1

Lockdown Feminization 2

The Female Species

How I Feminized My Husband

Maid To Serve

Feminized By My Wife

A Sissy Cuckold Husband 1

A Sissy Cuckold Husband 2

Becoming Joanne Boxset

Feminized and Pretty 1

Feminized and Pretty 2

Feminized and Pretty 3

The Reluctant Housemaid

An Accidental Girl

The Girl Within

A Sister-In-Law's Law

The Woman's World

A Very Dominant Woman

Her Toy

Becoming Joanne 1

Becoming Joanne 2

- **Becoming Joanne 3**
- **Feminization is Compulsory**
- **The New Assistant**

Printed in Great Britain
by Amazon